THE LION OF ANJOU

The Medieval Saga Series
Book Four

David Field

SAPERE BOOKS

THE LION OF ANJOU

Published by Sapere Books.

24 Trafalgar Road, Ilkley, LS29 8HH,
United Kingdom

saperebooks.com

ISBN: 978-1-80055-721-5

I

A wedding ceremony that was destined to shape the future of several nations was being conducted in secret. The chosen location was the Cathedral of St Peter, Poitiers, whose construction had been instigated by the woman who was now standing before its high altar to take her second set of wedding vows. It was 18th May 1152, and very few outside the immediate bridal party knew what was about to take place.

The bride was Eleanor, Duchess of Aquitaine and Countess of Poitou in her own right. At thirty years of age she was eleven years older than the groom, and she had until only two months previously been the Queen of France. The groom was destined to become King of England, and was already, thanks to his father's legacy, Duke of Normandy and Count of Anjou. He was Henry Plantagenet, the bride's third cousin, and he felt lust combined with territorial ambition as he was obliged to look upward in order to lock eyes with her.

Eleanor was breathtakingly beautiful, with auburn tresses cascading down the back of her bridal gown. She was also blessed with a slim figure, while Henry was stocky, ruddy-faced, red-haired, athletic and vigorous in appearance, in stark contrast to Eleanor's former first husband.

Seen from a personal and territorial perspective, it was a match made in Heaven. Between them, Eleanor and Henry would rule over a massive swathe of territories that ran, unbroken, from the borders with Flanders to the east, to the Atlantic shores in the west. Their combined lands of Normandy, Anjou, Maine, Aquitaine and Poitou would command all the Channel ports except those in Brittany. They would also stretch south all the way to the Vexin, the border country with the Île-de-France over which Louis VII reigned with covetous eyes on the territorial riches of his northern neighbours.

But from a religious and moral point of view, the Devil was behind this union. Henry, at only nineteen, was already a dedicated whoremaster to whom no woman was forbidden. He had a passion for hunting, fighting and carousing, and had sired several bastards. His temper was unpredictable and violent, and he did not take kindly to having his desires thwarted. But Eleanor, allegedly, was more than a match for him in her determination to get her own way.

She had been raised in the Court of Poitiers, where the much vaunted 'courtly love' was a polite euphemism for promiscuity at a noble level. She had proved to be wilful, headstrong, resentful of parental restraint and impatient to experience more than a modest region south-west of the Loire could offer by way of diversion. Almost as an act of rebellion she had consented to be married, at the tender age of fifteen, to the second son of Louis the Fat of France, who in a short space of time had become Louis VII. He had been destined for the Church until his older brother, the heir apparent Philip, had died, but Louis lived his subsequent years as if already ordained, with celibacy high on his personal agenda.

Little wonder that the affections of his libidinous queen were apt to wander, but it was not so much the fact that she strayed from her marital vows that scandalised the French court as the identities of those with whom she allegedly transgressed. Most notably, and most recently, ugly rumours had been circulating of an incestuous affair between Eleanor and her own uncle, Raymond of Poitiers, Prince of Antioch, during the ill-fated Second Crusade that Louis and Eleanor had embarked upon in an attempt to recapture Jerusalem from the Turks. Eleanor's strident protests at being forcibly removed from Antioch by her husband in order to proceed towards Jerusalem only added fuel to the fire of prurient speculation, but it was a matter of note that Eleanor was by then campaigning for the dissolution of her marriage to Louis on the grounds of consanguinity, given that they were fourth cousins.

The consanguinity issue had not, however, dissuaded Eleanor from marriage to Henry Plantagenet, to whom she was even more closely related. Of greater concern to Louis had been the failure of Eleanor to produce any male heirs to continue the Capetian dynasty into another generation; instead they had only two daughters, Marie and Alix. Louis may also have been embarrassed by Eleanor's growing reputation for gracing noble beds other than his, and in March of that year he had consented to the annulment. Eleanor had been once again free to rule her inherited lands of Aquitaine and Poitou without husbandly interference. She was also free to remarry, and the speed with which she had become the far from blushing bride on this warm and sunny day in May had also set tongues wagging.

Henry had first laid eyes on Eleanor the previous year, in the French palace located in the Île de la Cité, when successfully persuading Louis to recognise him as Duke of Normandy in succession to his father Geoffrey of Anjou, who had died shortly thereafter. Having seen her, he'd been unable look away, and it was believed that Henry's subsequent disappearances without notice for weeks at a time were in order to hold illicit liaisons with Eleanor. There had clearly been some exchange of communications between the two that had led to the clandestine ceremony that was now taking place

— one that would be almost guaranteed to launch a bloody war.

For one thing, it was a huge, and very public, insult to Louis of France. Perhaps more importantly, it created a massive power block to Louis' north and seemed destined to extinguish any succession rights of Louis' daughters Marie and Alix to Aquitaine. All it would take would be the birth of a male heir to Henry and Eleanor, and the odds were very much in favour of that, given the sensual proclivities of the bride and groom.

Little wonder that there were no invited guests, no proud proclamations of the impending nuptials, and virtually no-one in attendance as the marriage vows were being exchanged. Not even Henry's mother was there, the redoubtable Matilda through whom Henry was confidently, and impatiently, expecting to inherit the crown of England, although even that claim was bitterly disputed.

For the past seventeen years, since the death of his grandfather Henry in 1135, Henry's mother Matilda had been locked in a never-ending, and occasionally bloody, internecine contest with her cousin Stephen of Blois over which of them had the right to the crown of England. Matilda, generally referred to as 'Maude', was the only surviving child of the deceased King Henry, and Stephen was his nephew, who had for a brief while been proclaimed by Henry as his heir. Barons on both sides of the Channel had been dragged into the conflict, until it had degenerated into a stalemate and they had begun warring with each other.

Maude had implied to the world that she had become exhausted and dispirited by her lack of success. Following the death of her husband Geoffrey of Anjou, she had retired to a priory on the outskirts of Caen, Normandy's traditional capital, leaving her son Henry to fight on, carrying the Angevin hopes on his battle banners. While Henry was fuming in the wings, plotting how to wrest the crown of England from an increasingly unpopular King Stephen, the last thing he needed was an attack from the south by an outraged Louis of France.

This was also the last thing desired by the grey-haired man now in his fifty-first year who was guarding the entrance doors to the cathedral along with three of his men, ensuring that no-one but those who had an unarguable right to be there could witness the ceremony. He was Richard, Earl of Chalfont, Henry's Captain of the Royal Guard, and one of the few allowed sufficiently close to Henry to know what he was likely to do next.

Not that Richard had any great regard for the man he had been all but forced to follow, with his evil temper and a stubborn recklessness that was likely to get them both killed. Richard had originally been seduced into siding with Stephen when he'd learned that his mother Emma had been Stephen's illegitimate half-sister, and that therefore Stephen was his uncle. Richard had been feeling particularly vulnerable at that time, having been dismissed from service at the Westminster Palace of the deceased King Henry by his own father, then Captain of the Palace Guard, following Richard's perceived incompetence in allowing his older sister Elinor to be seduced by a romantic adventurer from the Vexin estate of Evreux. The outcome of the brief affair had been the birth of twin sons, Alain and William, whom Elinor had been forced to abandon. The boys had been confined to an orphanage in Norfolk and had never met their father.

In return for throwing in his lot with Stephen, Richard had been granted the estate of Chalfont, along with the earldom and the plump widow Agnes, both of which came with it. Then, conversely, his own family's immediate interests had dragged him into Maude's camp when she and his sister Elinor, who was employed as Maude's senior lady and companion, had been trapped inside Oxford Castle when it was besieged by Stephen's troops. Richard had staged a daring and successful escape operation which made him a traitor to Stephen's cause. He had then taken what seemed like an easy option at the time, namely an invitation by Maude to travel to Normandy in order to keep a watchful eye on the teenage Henry, who seemed fated to die by his own recklessness unless suitably restrained.

Although elevated to his current status by a grudgingly grateful, but definitely needful, Henry, Richard was now stuck between two hard choices — desert Henry and scurry furtively back to England, risking a traitor's death at Stephen's hands, or remain where he was and take the verbal abuse and perpetual ingratitude from the arrogant and ambitious prince who was standing in front of the altar with the expression of someone who had just been handed the moon and the stars.

Following the ceremony, Henry and Eleanor were escorted back to the castle at Poitiers, where they intended to reside temporarily while Henry decided how best to pursue his ambition to remove Stephen from the throne of England. This in itself created problems for Richard to deal with, since the ancient fortress that brought back such happy childhood memories for Eleanor was seething with resentment and discontent from querulous locals. They were too used to governing themselves in the almost permanent absence of any feudal overlord, and they were not about to be deprived of their virtual self-rule by a man barely out of his teens who was crude, aggressive, seemingly uncultured and 'foreign', even if he *had* succeeded in bedding their own senior lady. In the opinion of many, Eleanor could have, and once had, done better for herself.

Louis of France responded to the insult by forming a coalition to thwart Henry's territorial ambitions. As part of this process he persuaded King Stephen of England, along with his son and declared heir Eustace, to stir up trouble for Henry in his own land, while the Counts of Champagne and Perche were ordered to harass Henry Plantagenet on his Normandy borders.

Stephen's contribution was to lay siege to Wallingford Castle, a strategic fortress overlooking one of the few fordable crossings of the Thames just west of London. It had been held by Henry's forces for many years, and it was key to his English ambitions. It was also worryingly close to Richard's estate in Buckinghamshire, and he was only too eager to obey Henry's next command once Louis' own failing health forced him to withdraw from his threatened campaign against Aquitaine, and the smattering of local uprisings fizzled out. Henry ordered all his available troops, including a worrying number of mercenaries, to cross the Channel under his command and lift the siege. Richard was informed that he was to accompany Henry, both to protect his person and to cast an experienced eye over Stephen's troops surrounding Wallingford. He was also granted grudging permission to visit his own estate on his way to Wallingford from Portsmouth when the invading force landed.

'I was wondering if you would ever return,' Agnes greeted Richard starchily as she welcomed him home with an eager hug that belied her critical words. 'King Stephen has been expecting Henry to invade, and I have continued to attend Court in order to learn what I could to your advantage — which means mine as well, I suppose.'

'And what have you learned?' Richard enquired as he led her back into the manor house, from which the aroma of newly baked bread was proving irresistible. 'I'll eat while you tell me what you can. Has Stephen been calling for my head?'

'He can barely call for silence these days,' Agnes advised him, 'given the riotous clamour that surrounds him, with barons in both his ears offering him competing advice. The Court has degenerated into a shambles, such that no-one seems to recall that my husband is known to be fighting for Henry of Anjou — except the ones who let it be known that when you invade they wish to join your side, in order to bring the uncertainty to an end. You should also know that Stephen has lost the support of the Church, and that Archbishop Theobald of Canterbury refused to crown Stephen's son Eustace as the next King of England, before he fled to Flanders for his own safety. Stephen and Theobald were reconciled only recently, but Theobald continues to cast public doubt on Stephen's claim to the throne. Most of the clerical offices are hanging vacant, and the only bishop who seems to enjoy Stephen's favour is his own brother Henry, Bishop of Winchester.'

'I can hardly relieve the siege of Wallingford with bell, book and candle,' Richard sneered as he ripped a large chunk from a loaf of bread that had just been delivered to the table, then muttered a curse as it burned his fingers.

Agnes frowned. 'You will give yourself a gripe if you eat that bread quickly when it has only just left the oven,' she admonished him. 'And I can only hope that your sexual needs are not so urgent, since it has been a long while and my ageing bones object to vigorous overuse. But it is not just the clergy who grow restless under Stephen.'

'Who else?'

'I was approached privily by your old master Hugh Bigod, who first of all cursed your memory as a deserter from Stephen's cause, then asked that he be called upon should Henry decide to put his sword arm where his mouth has been these past few years. He claimed also to be speaking for Ranulf of Chester, who I personally would not trust to lie straight in bed. However, it seems that they would welcome the chance to pay homage to "King Henry" in due course.'

'You are very fortunate to have been able to attend Court without being seized and imprisoned,' Richard reminded her, secretly impressed by both her courage and her acumen. 'I have no doubt that if he got his hands on me, King Stephen would have me hanged from the palace walls as a warning to other traitors.'

Agnes leaned down and kissed the top of his head. 'I had no other calls on my time, and I was obviously lacking company and diversion during your lengthy absence. I also wished to learn if you would be in any immediate danger were you to return, but as I already advised you it would seem that the king needs all the friends he can collect around him these days, and he is much distracted. I doubt that he even remembers that you and I are married.'

Richard sighed. 'Unfortunately, Duke Henry seems to suffer from the same malady. He is so obsessed with having me by his side while he pursues his dream of conquering England that he forgets that I have a wife and estate of my own back here.'

'But you are not by his side now, so where is he?'

'He is at the old royal hunting lodge at Stockbridge, which is only one day's ride from where we landed, and two days' ride from here. It is also close to the Treasury at Winchester. We may lay siege to that first, depending on what I can advise him regarding the size of Stephen's force at Wallingford.'

'I can tell you that much,' Agnes smiled, 'since I have been riding there almost weekly, along with two of our armed attendants, Giles and Edmund. We estimate the besieging force to be several thousand strong.'

Richard rose from the table and hugged Agnes tightly to him. 'What a wife for a fighting man such as I to be blessed with! What would I do without you?'

'It is what you intend to do *with* me that concerns me at this moment,' she smiled up at him enticingly. 'But mind what I said about the frailty of my bones.'

II

As Richard had himself admitted to the main hall of the hunting lodge at Stockbridge, Henry was deep in a murmured conversation with a man whose face was somehow familiar to Richard, but whom he felt sure he had never met. Henry looked away briefly from the conversation to welcome Richard back gruffly, adding, 'How fares your wife?'

'Middling well, thank you,' Richard replied. 'You owe her a considerable debt of thanks. Not only has she been keeping a watchful eye on Stephen's forces surrounding Wallingford, but she has been attending Court, at considerable risk to herself, and was able to advise me that several of the leading barons are waiting to throw in their lot with you. She made mention in particular of Ranulf of Chester.'

The visitor made a derisive noise, and turned in order to spit into the rushes.

Henry grinned and effected the introductions. 'You really *did* make a very poor diplomat before you finally realised what you do best. Allow me to introduce Robert de Beaumont, Earl of Leicester, who has also offered me his considerable armed force in order to topple Stephen from his usurped throne.'

Robert smiled coldly as he addressed Richard. 'You were at one time in league with my brother Waleran, before you both changed sides. As for Ranulf, he is a treacherous bastard who seized my estates in Dorset and handed them to Robert of Gloucester. But following Robert's death I got them back by sheer force of arms, and in addition I took Ranulf's fortress at Mountsorrel. We have been waging war on each other for the past three years, and now the slimy bastard seeks peace terms with Henry, after supporting the usurper for many years?'

Now Richard realised why the face was so familiar, even though this was his first glimpse of it. The two brothers were almost identical in appearance, and he recalled his last encounter with Waleran. 'I last saw your brother in Normandy, when he was attempting to wean me back to Stephen's cause. He was at that time planning on going on crusade — did he do so?'

'He did, and he survived, but unfortunately he became too close with Louis of France, to whom he is bound for his Vexin estate in Meulan. To make matters worse he has married a sister of de Montfort, which makes his loyalties doubly suspect. It has been left to me to preserve the family's honour and estates here in England.'

'What saw you of Stephen's force at Wallingford?' Henry interrupted grumpily. 'Or did you leave *that* entirely to your wife as well?'

'I sat for some time on a hill overlooking the castle on my first day's journey back here,' Richard replied icily, 'and I would estimate that there are at least four thousand armed men surrounding it. No doubt they are busily engaged in pillaging the surrounding countryside while we dawdle here.'

'All the more reason to do as I suggest,' Robert observed with a smirk.

Henry nodded. 'Perhaps, but let us see what Richard has to say.'

'He will not be leading your army,' Robert reminded him sharply.

'Indeed he will not, but he will be guarding my person while you lead the attack. Richard is an experienced strategist, so tell him what you suggested to me.'

Robert adopted a condescending smile as he explained. 'Stephen has unwisely loaded all his dice and thrown them at the one target which is perhaps impregnable. Wallingford can well withstand the siege for several more weeks by my calculations, and it is my advice, born of experience of years in the field, that we draw some of Stephen's force further west. When they are committed, we sneak back north, then pass quickly through my Midland estates and relieve the siege from the north, once Stephen's ranks there are greatly reduced.'

Richard considered this briefly. 'My first thought is that you would need to travel very quickly in order to double back by such a circuitous route. You would also need provisions for a large army on the move.'

'I command all the estates north and east of Bristol, and we could proceed through several of them before turning south once more,' de Beaumont replied gloatingly. 'It's a fast road to London by that route, and it was a good harvest, so the barns are full. Given the time of year, the tracks should be frozen hard, so that we could anticipate making twenty miles a day.'

'So how do you propose to draw Stephen westward?' Richard asked.

'Malmesbury. Stephen has been using it for some time as the base for his defence of the port of Bristol, and his men have incurred the wrath of its citizens by raiding the surrounding estates for provisions. They are in permanent discord with the abbot of the nearby abbey, and I have no doubt that were we to lay siege to the town, half of those within its walls would be delighted to open its gates to us. Then when Stephen marches west to reclaim it, we move swiftly north, and circle round him back to Wallingford.'

'It will take us perhaps two weeks to march a sizeable party of armed men in a semi-circle such as you describe,' Richard objected, 'whereas Stephen can head back east to reinforce the siege of Wallingford in a matter of days.'

'Only if he knows what we are about,' Robert grinned. 'It is my proposal that we retreat across the Avon as if making for Wales, deceiving Stephen into believing that we intend to join up with Ranulf in Chester. Instead, we follow the north bank of the Avon until we pick up the track to Cirencester and head north-east. Cirencester remains loyal to me, because it knows what is good for it, and from there we skirt around the north side of Oxford. Then we shall be upon Wallingford in just over one more day.'

'We would probably be passing by my own estate, if not actually through it,' Richard advised them both with a look of alarm.

'Here's hoping that your wife keeps a fine table, then,' said Henry. 'If you have no better objection than that, I propose that we ready our troops to depart at daybreak tomorrow.'

'Where are your men?' Richard asked Robert.

'Eating the locals out of house and home. There are several thousand of them imposed on every household in a ten-mile radius of here, and my commanders can round them up in a matter of hours. I shall set about that now, if I might be excused?'

'Do you trust him?' Richard asked Henry once the doors had closed behind Robert.

Henry frowned. 'Do I have a choice? But from what you tell me, there will be others riding to my support. Your wife is indeed to be commended, if she has been bending the leading barons to my cause. It is a great benefit in life to have the support of a loyal wife. Mine remains at home in Poitiers, but in her latest despatch she gave me the glad tidings that she is with child.'

'Congratulations,' Richard smiled, since it seemed to be expected. 'But I did not mean to convey the impression that my wife Agnes has been actively soliciting armed support for your cause. As I understand it, the barons in question approached her. There was also mention of Hugh Bigod of Norwich, who I served under in my former days. If that be correct, then we shall be able to secure most of East Anglia.'

'We have yet to rescue Wallingford,' Henry reminded him. 'And before that, we need to secure Malmesbury. Your task will be to ensure my safety, of course, so you will remain with me to the rear of any fighting. No heroic ventures of your own, is that understood? At your age that would not be a wise action anyway.'

'You place your personal safety in the hands of an old man?' Richard challenged.

Henry nodded. 'An old man who knows how to select and command men, certainly. Now, go to your rest. We have an early start on the morrow.'

It almost went to plan. Within a week they were outside the walls of Malmesbury and raiding local estates for the provisions they required in order to keep a modestly sized army fed and watered. The men glowered up at the defenders on the city walls and hurled the occasional missile over them to remind those trapped inside that they were under siege. As anticipated, Stephen pulled some of his forces from the ongoing siege of Wallingford and marched west. Then it began to snow heavily as Henry's force crossed the Avon and sat shouting abuse across the water at the new arrivals.

It was obvious even to someone with only a passing familiarity with warfare that either army could have crossed the relatively shallow and narrow ford to engage the other, but preservation from the bitter cold took priority. On the third day, a messenger sent by Henry returned with the heartening news that Stephen was prepared to withdraw if Henry did. Since this allowed Henry to travel north into the now friendly territory of the Earl of Leicester, he regarded the offer as a generous one. By the end of the week, he was commodiously installed inside Warwick Castle as the guest of Robert de Beaumont.

This left open the issue of whether or not Stephen's forces had taken advantage of the temporary truce in order to reinforce the siege at Wallingford. Richard persuaded Henry that since he was safely behind some of the strongest castle walls in England it might be the appropriate time for Richard to return to his estate, from which he could closely observe events to the east, on the fordable crossing of the Thames that made Wallingford such a key fortress.

On his return home, he found Agnes confined to her chamber with an ague she had acquired during the recent cold weather. Given that she was now in her mid-fifties, this was not something to be taken lightly. Richard insisted on spending most of his time at her bedside, urging her to swallow the endless beef stew prepared by Janet the cook, along with potions from the new infirmarian of the local abbey, who had replaced the one who had ministered to Richard's father on his deathbed.

'I little thought,' Agnes commented as she began to show signs of recovery, 'when I agreed to King Stephen's suggestion that I marry an eager young adventurer who was also his nephew, that he would turn out to be a kind and solicitous man who would comfort me in my old age.'

'You are little older than me,' Richard smiled as he squeezed her hand, 'and *I* little thought that I would learn so much about the carnal arts.'

'Away with you!' Agnes giggled, then coughed. 'You make me sound like a witch. But I own that it also came as a pleasant and totally unexpected bonus. You're really quite good at it — are you sure that I was your first?'

'First *and* last,' Richard assured her. 'Now, get some sleep, for I must ride to Wallingford again tomorrow, and I wish to say my goodbyes at daybreak — just in case.'

'Just in case what?' Agnes demanded, a look of alarm on her face. 'You are not to try anything dangerous, do you understand?'

Richard chuckled. 'Henry said much the same when I left him. I shall obey both duke and wife and ensure that my old bones are not left bleaching under the walls of Wallingford. Once you are back on your feet you may be playing host to royalty, so occupy your mind with that terrifying thought, rather than the possible demise of a husband. Henry likes his meat, so ensure that the larder is well stocked.'

It was obvious that in less than a week Stephen had done what Richard would have done in his place, and had taken his men back to Wallingford. The force now surrounding the castle walls came close to once again equalling those available to Henry, and if the siege was to be lifted it would have to be soon. Richard was therefore very relieved, once he returned home after reporting the current situation to Henry in Warwick, to find that Agnes had risen from her bed to issue instructions in her familiar strident tones to everyone employed on the estate. She was clearly back to her old self, a point she reinforced by yelling at Richard to remove his boots before entering the manor house, and only then moving forward to hug him.

'Henry has sent messengers ahead of you, to warn of his imminent arrival,' she said, flustered and clearly nervous. 'I've ordered the slaughter of five of our best beasts — will that suffice?'

'For Henry himself, perhaps,' Richard replied, 'but we do not know how many others will accompany him.'

That doubt was resolved the following day, as the warm spring sun rose to its full height, and the clatter of hooves on the cobbles of the stable yard announced the arrival of six men at arms, followed immediately by Henry, riding alongside the Earl of Leicester.

Richard walked out to welcome their honoured guests, and introduced Agnes. 'My dear wife, and your fervent supporter at Stephen's court.'

Henry dismounted with a smile and took her extended hand in order to kiss it. 'Your husband speaks highly of your efforts in receiving the promised support of some of the strongest barons in the land. But he said nothing of your cooking, so I imagine that you leave that to others.'

Two days of feasting, fortunately with only Henry and de Beaumont at board in the manor house itself, were followed by a further day of strategic talks, at the conclusion of which it was agreed that no time should be wasted in attempting to lift the siege of Wallingford. The following day the messengers were dispatched to those local alehouses, cottages and holy houses that had been the involuntary hosts of the invading army, and on the fifth day Henry rode out in pride of place at the head of his force, with Richard riding alongside to his left, and de Beaumont to his right.

As they approached from the north, it was obvious that Stephen had taken advantage of the delay caused by the adverse weather in order to restore his siege forces to full strength, and they were encamped all around the walls of Wallingford Castle. The approach of Henry and his army across the river meadows was met with a hoarse challenge from the first line of Stephen's force, followed by general jeering from the remaining ranks, along with crude insults and invitations to fight and die. Then from the front rank emerged a knight on horseback, riding alone and carrying a plain white flag. He slowly crossed the uneven ground between the two armies, then pulled gently on the reins in order to remain stationary almost a hundred yards from the front line of Henry's force.

From the top of the slight rise to the rear, Henry gave a grunt of displeasure and enquired, 'What is that fool about, and why does he display only a white battle banner? Where is his livery?'

Richard tried not to chuckle, such was his relief at this promising turn of events. 'The white flag denotes that he comes in peace. He may even be bearing surrender terms from King Stephen.'

'So what are we supposed to do?'

'Send someone out to meet him, in order to enquire as to his business.'

'Since you would seem to know what is going on, *you* go. But if he brings merely a request from his master that we withdraw, tell him we refuse!'

A few minutes later Richard brought his own mount alongside that of the man with the white flag, who introduced himself as William d'Aubigny, Earl of Lincoln. 'I come with proposed truce terms from King Stephen,' he added.

'I have been sent out from the ranks by Duke Henry of Normandy,' Richard advised him, 'who disputes your master's right to call himself the King of England. Be that as it may, what does he propose?'

'That you disperse from here, and that Henry and my master meet again at a mutually agreed place, in order to negotiate a lasting peace.'

Richard smiled slowly. 'I can only assume that King Stephen feels his position here to be weak, and I certainly would not wish to be hemmed in between an advancing foe and a sturdy set of castle walls. I feel sure that Henry will reject your proposal, particularly after I point out to him that he has the decided advantage.'

William d'Aubigny nodded towards the gentle slope that led down to the rear ranks of Henry's force. At the top, more battle banners could be seen, prominent among which were those bearing the blue heraldic device of the House of Blois. 'Yours has now become the force trapped between two opposing armies,' he gloated. 'Your master will no doubt be advised by those who understand these things that retreat would be a wise option in the situation into which his folly has led him. When he comes to his senses, tell him that King Stephen will await him in Winchester a week from today.'

With that, he turned his horse's head and rode back into the ranks of the besieging force. Richard kicked his horse into a canter in his urgency to persuade Henry that if he did not remove himself and his men from the field, they would be slaughtered. The wild curses that followed this revelation could be heard throughout the ranks, but there were smiles on the faces of those who realised the peril they had been in when the order was given by de Beaumont that they were to retreat in an orderly fashion back across the river meadow and onto the track to distant Oxford.

III

A week later, Henry sat with de Beaumont on one side and Richard on the other in a large marquee on the grassy ground before the walls of Winchester, awaiting the peace delegation from King Stephen.

'If he does not yield the crown immediately, I shall gather more forces in Normandy and blow him all the way to the Scottish border!' Henry growled as he swallowed the dregs of his third mug of wine and gestured for the page to refill it.

De Beaumont glanced nervously across at Richard, then steeled himself to offer advice. 'You are about to become a father, Henry, and should it be a boy you will no doubt wish to leave him a rich legacy of land, just as your father did for you. Stephen has two sons of his own, Eustace and William, and were he to surrender the throne today, he would be disinheriting them both. His proposed terms will no doubt make provision for them, which means that it is unlikely that you will leave this tent as King of England.'

'We may just as well leave now, then! Damn Stephen of Blois! A curse on him, and a murrain on his sons! What he will not yield by treaty, I shall take from him by force!'

Henry hurled his wine mug to the ground, and was in the process of rising to his feet when the tent flap was opened by an armed attendant, and in walked three men in clerical garb. Ignoring Henry's outburst, they walked to the table that had obviously been installed for their use and unrolled several scrolls of parchment. Then the most senior of them, and the older man by twenty years or so, smiled and stood in front of his table. His attendants took inkpots and quills from the bags they had carried in, and sat awaiting further instructions.

The newcomer smiled as he recognised Richard. 'We have met before, I believe. If I am correct, then my brother the king — and your uncle — sends loving greetings, and wishes me to assure you that there is no ill will from his side.'

'Who is this poxy priest?' Henry demanded as he made no further move to leave.

'He is the younger brother of Stephen of Blois,' Richard advised him. 'His name is also Henry, and the last I heard he was the Bishop of Winchester. As you will have deduced for yourself, he is also my uncle.'

'We can save the family reunions until later,' Henry insisted tersely as he glared at Richard, 'although had I known of your lineage, I would not even have allowed you to turn the spit in my kitchens.'

'I cannot be held responsible for what my mother did with my father any more than you can,' Richard replied angrily. 'The relationship is hardly close anyway, since my mother was the illegitimate sister of the two brothers from Blois. My father, who was thought of highly by your mother, even though she knew of his dalliance with a daughter of a rival house, never once swerved in his loyalty to the Lady Maude, and my sister, as you know, served as her companion. It was your mother who bid me to serve your cause, and I do not believe that I have given you any ground for suspicion as to my loyalties. Perhaps we might be better employed learning of Stephen's proposals.'

Henry's face had reddened in anger at Richard's defiant words, but this last observation caused him to hold back from any further insult. He turned to the Bishop of Winchester with raised eyebrows. 'So what does your usurping dog of a brother propose?'

The bishop bowed his head meekly. 'I do not come with proposals, my lord. I come to seek instruction as to what *you* might have in mind to ensure a lasting peace. The Archbishop Theobald of Canterbury is performing a similar service for my brother, and the intention is that the archbishop and myself will act as the go-betweens.'

'And why should we agree to any peace terms?' Henry demanded, still far from placated. 'Why should we not continue until one of us is dead?'

'Because,' came the gentle reply, 'many others will die in the process, and as a man of God I cannot sit idly by and allow that to happen, if it be within my power to prevent it. Then there is the matter of the nation itself, which will hardly be worth fighting over if your conflict with King Stephen continues. The people are starving, the barons are warring among themselves, the Treasury is all but bare and God has abandoned the Church. His Holiness the Pope is on the verge of imposing an interdict on the entire nation, which would open the door further to Satan, who has already blasted this country with plagues, famine and ungodliness.'

'A pretty speech,' Henry sneered, 'but does your brother intend to yield me the throne? If not, then the chaos will continue, and the ultimate loser will be the House of Blois.'

'With respect, my lord, the ultimate loser would be the land of England,' the bishop murmured as he lowered his head to reveal the full extent of his tonsure. 'Would you wish to inherit the crown of a wasteland cursed by God?'

'And who has created this unhappy state of affairs?' Henry challenged him with a reddening face.

The bishop frowned. 'Both of you — Stephen *and* yourself. And before that, Stephen and your mother. We are not here, the archbishop and myself, in order to mediate between yourself and your distant cousin — we are here to rescue England from *both* of you. So what would you require, in order for you to disband your army and let your people heal themselves?'

'The crown of England, no less.'

'Now or later?'

'Of what use would "later" be, when Stephen has had time to bequeath it to his sons, just as my grandfather bequeathed it to him, only to regret his action when my mother was free to accept it, which was his first wish?'

'So you wish to become king immediately, and for the royal sons to be disinherited?'

'Did I not just say so?'

'And if King Stephen wishes to live out his days as King of England?'

'Then he will be destined never to live a single one of those days in peace. No doubt even now he is insisting to the Archbishop of Canterbury that he will only accept my immediate withdrawal from what he believes to be his nation as his condition for making a permanent peace. For you see, we are both stubborn men, and we have both come too far to step backwards.'

'Perhaps God will enter your hearts as you contemplate your souls' destinies,' the bishop replied as he made the sign of the cross. 'And so I say *pax vobiscum*, and take my leave for the time being. I hope to return on the morrow, once I have spoken with the archbishop.'

'You may find yourself speaking to an empty tent,' Henry replied sternly. He then made a point of turning his back on the clerical party as they bowed quietly back under the tent flap. 'I think I made my position abundantly clear,' he said to Richard and de Beaumont in a tone that was part assertion and part a request for confirmation.

Richard was the first to reply. 'As you yourself observed, my lord, Stephen is hardly likely to agree to rise from his throne and wave you into it. We must consider some lesser position to adopt if we are to end this constant warfare for the sake of England.'

'It has been Stephen's inability to govern a nation that has created this mess,' Henry insisted hotly, 'which explains why so many of the leading barons are now looking to me to clean it up. Those who remain loyal to Stephen only do so in order to retain their estates and positions of power in a midden of their own making. England needs me!'

'And it might yet be possible for them to have you as their king,' de Beaumont replied quietly. When Henry shot him a hard and disbelieving look, he explained. 'We *must* make some concession, Henry. Stephen is hardly likely to walk away after enjoying the privileges of monarchy for so many years, and if we cannot come to some arrangement with him, then we shall be destined to roam the countryside of England until his death. In the meantime, you remain vulnerable to Louis of France in your southern estates.'

This caused Henry to pause, and Robert expanded his argument.

'Stephen is approaching sixty years of age, whereas you are barely over twenty. Should he be persuaded to name you as his heir, you would not need to wait for much longer for nature to come to your aid. In the meantime, you may reinforce your position in Normandy, Maine, Aquitaine and Poitiers and watch your family steadily increase.'

'And what of the sons, Eustace and William?' Henry objected. 'What would be their likely reaction to such a dispossession? Surely we would be back where my mother started when she herself was cut from the succession, and the royal sons would continue to wage war against me, would they not?'

'Not if they are formally dispossessed as part of a perpetual peace treaty sworn on oath,' Robert suggested. 'God knows we have enough clergymen in attendance to make that possible.'

Henry swirled the wine around his cup, then fixed Richard with an enquiring stare. 'What say you?'

Richard half bowed. 'My main duty, as I understand it, is to preserve you from death, whether at the hand of an enemy, or through your own rashness. Were you to accept the crown of England under such terms as Robert suggests, and retire to your estates across the Channel, then my task would be much easier. And as Robert reminds you, you have a growing family to nurture and provide for. In due course, you will no doubt have a son to whom to bequeath England in your turn, thus ensuring that the House of Blois can never reclaim it.'

Henry's brow furrowed with the effort of even considering concession, but he could not avoid the sense of what was being proposed. Then the reference to Eleanor's impending lying-in finally tipped the scale, and he grunted a reluctant agreement.

'I doubt that Stephen could be persuaded to disinherit his own sons, but for the sake of argument I will go along with what you suggest. But if those prating clerics return on the morrow with some weak proposal that denies me the throne of England forever, I shall invite them to eat it. And now it must surely be time for dinner — did you send men to slaughter some of those fine deer we passed on the road several days past?'

Satisfied that the door to some sort of settlement remained at least partly open, Richard stepped out of the tent in search of fresh air. The sun was fierce overhead, and the leather jerkin that lay over his shirt was beginning to heat up, so he unfastened it and slung it over his shoulder as he walked towards the stream that supplied the town of Winchester by means of a craftily constructed conduit that conveyed it under the walls. His military mind was busily noting that it made the city vulnerable to the cutting off or poisoning of its water supply, while creating a weak point for besieging men at arms, when he became aware of a young monk kneeling by the bank of the stream in order to wash a cassock.

It took him a second to realise that the profile of the young man was familiar before the monk turned as he heard the approach of Richard's boots. He rose to his feet, the dripping cassock held firmly in one hand, and the two men locked eyes.

Richard broke the silence. 'Are you by any chance from the Abbey of Ely?'

'I was — once,' the monk smiled in reply. 'In fact, I was educated there. But now I serve the Archbishop of Canterbury.'

'Your name is Alain, and you have a twin brother called William?'

'In truth, while I have in recent years adopted the clerical name of "Brother Benedict", my birth name *was* Alain, and my brother is indeed named William. Your face is familiar to me, although it was younger when I last saw it.'

'In the Cathedral School at Ely, when I came to visit that final time. My name was once Richard Walsingham, although like you I chose to change it. I am now entitled "Richard, Earl of Chalfont". But in either capacity I am your uncle. Is it permitted for an uncle to embrace a nephew in holy orders?'

'Whether it is or not, I do not believe that you have earned that right, since you conspired in our abandonment by our parents.'

'They had little choice, Alain, each for their own reason,' Richard advised him. 'Your mother was not then married to your father — although she was later — and was in service to the Lady Maude, the mother of Henry of Anjou who is currently invading, and who I serve. As for your father, he was a gallant young adventurer from the southern borders of Normandy, and was obliged to return in order to do homage to Louis of France, England's long-time enemy. He did not even know of your existence when he left the Court at Westminster.'

'But we were, nevertheless, born out of wedlock?'

'Yes, you were, but only because circumstances prevented any marriage. I can assure you that your mother suffered deeply from your absence in her life.'

'She was so overcome by conscience that she sent you in her stead to oversee our welfare?' Alain enquired sceptically.

Richard was obliged to nod in concession. 'Do not judge her too harshly — she was, after all, my sister, and I loved her dearly. Sadly, I have to advise you that both your parents were taken by a pestilence that ran riot through Normandy several years past. But what brings you here, in the train of Archbishop Theobald?'

'He required clerks to record the details of any peace accord that may be reached between King Stephen and your master, so myself and Brother Ambrose were loaned to him from the scriptorium in which we work as part of the congregation of the monastery attached to the cathedral. But it would seem from what we learned from the Bishop of Winchester that Henry of Anjou will accept nothing other than the crown of England on his head before he will cease the warfare.'

Richard looked carefully behind him and lowered his voice before leaning towards Alain. 'There may be a way around this impasse, which your archbishop should know of.'

'Continue, please,' Alain replied, 'since England has suffered enough from Godless warmongers.'

'Henry might be persuaded to withdraw to his estates across the Channel were Stephen to name him as his heir. That way, Stephen may live out his days as king, and Henry may be assured that England will one day be his. The only obstacle to that would seem to be the existence of Stephen's two sons, who might consider that they have a prior right to succeed.'

'As indeed they do,' Alain conceded as he thought deeply for a moment. 'But what if Henry were *also* a son of Stephen?'

'But he is not.'

'Not a natural son, of course. But what if Stephen were to adopt him?'

'Would that be possible?'

'I would obviously need to seek the counsel of the archbishop, but I see no ground for objection. Adoptions are quite common among the nobility, given the regrettable amount of illegitimacy that disgraces the nation.'

'You will carry my thoughts back to Archbishop Theobald?'

'Indeed I will, and I thank you for the opportunity to prove my worth to him.'

'Are you sufficiently indebted to me to advise me of the current welfare of your twin brother?'

'Since you are his uncle as well as mine, I can hardly refuse. When we left the abbey school, we both went on to study at

Oxford. We were advised that you had paid our tuition fees — is that correct?'

'It is, although the money came from your parents. But while you clearly took holy orders, I assume that William did not?'

'Indeed not, since he is too enamoured of matters of the flesh. He set out to seek a career in the practice of law, and when last he paid me a visit at Canterbury he was in the service of the chancellor, who is also the Dean of York. I had half hoped to meet up with him again here, since the Treasury is still housed at Winchester, is it not? But so far I have not had the opportunity.'

'If you do, will you arrange for me to meet with him also?' Richard asked eagerly.

Alain frowned. 'That would not be wise, I suggest. William serves as a common lawyer inside one of the most senior and important offices in the nation. How would it be for his advancement were he known to be related to a man who serves England's enemy?'

Richard sighed. 'I must accept that, of course, but hopefully it will be otherwise once I serve your new king. You may help to bring that about, after what I have disclosed to you in confidence.'

'For which I thank you once more, but now I must return to my duties,' Alain replied. He turned to go, then added, almost as an afterthought, 'If we do not meet again, many thanks for what you did for us in the past.'

The air was tense around the breakfast board inside Henry's hunting lodge at Stockbridge the following morning as Richard and Robert chose their words carefully to avoid provoking their master's unpredictable temper.

Finally, it was Henry who came bluntly to the point. 'If we are offered anything less than the crown at this morning's meeting, we walk away, is that understood?'

'It is,' de Beaumont muttered as he carved more cheese from the block.

When Henry looked demandingly at Richard from under raised eyebrows, he ventured a suggestion.

'What will be your response if you are offered the crown ahead of the royal sons?'

'Your meaning?'

'Well, you said yourself that Stephen is hardly likely to wish to vacate the throne during his lifetime. As Robert reminded you yesterday, you are a young man in the prime of life, whereas Stephen has seen his better years.'

'So what?' Henry countered grumpily. 'We have no idea how many years of life Stephen may have left to him, and what man could be persuaded to disinherit his own sons?'

'My point,' Richard continued patiently and softly, 'is that we need to offer some compromise. Stephen currently occupies the throne, and you wish to. You cannot share a reign between you, but if Stephen could be persuaded to make you his heir then you would both achieve what you wish. The only losers would be the royal sons, but each of you would be seen to have given something by way of compromise.'

Henry shot him a suspicious look as he waved for more wine. 'Do you know something of Stephen's intentions that you are withholding from me? He may be your uncle, but I am your master, and will in due course — by some means or other — be your king. So what are you keeping back?'

'Nothing — sire,' Richard assured him, throwing in the title in the hope of softening Henry's mood. 'It is simply the compromise that I would offer were I in Stephen's place.'

'Well, you are not, and I doubt that the slimy rat would even go that far.'

'But if he does, we must be prepared,' Richard suggested.

'The only thing we must be prepared for at this moment is to ride for over two hours to a meeting that may last only a minute. See to it that the steward ensures that sufficient food and wine accompany us.'

There was the hint of a contented smile on the face of the Bishop of Winchester as he and his two clerks bowed their way to the table in the centre of the marquee and unpacked their few items. An ominous silence was broken only by a few muttered words of ecclesiastical Latin as the bishop made the sign of the cross, cleared his throat, and announced what he had been instructed to report.

'My brother concedes that you harbour a justifiable grievance that your grandfather preferred his claim to your mother's in the matter of the crown of England. He also concedes that the late King Henry had for some time hoped that his successor might be the Lady Matilda. However, he suggests that both of your grandfather's wishes might be fulfilled were you to be left the throne after his death, and to this end he offers that in return for your withdrawal back to your provinces across the Channel, he will make you his heir to England.'

'A hollow promise, while he has two sons,' Henry snarled. 'A cheap trick to get us off his back. Were I to agree to that, and were his sons to lay claim to the crown upon Stephen's death, we would be back to where this whole sorry business began. Two competing claims, two armies, and England ravaged beyond recall. It was you who claimed to have the welfare of the nation as your first priority — what you propose would serve merely to perpetuate the bloodshed into the next generation.'

The bishop smiled and nodded. 'That consideration was also foremost in my brother's mind, and to leave no-one in doubt as to where the crown is to go on his death, he offers to adopt you as another royal son.'

In the stunned silence, Henry could be seen counting on his fingers. He looked up with a smirk. 'Do I really give the impression that I am so stupid, my lord bishop? Eustace is older than me by two years, and the law dictates that estates go to older sons.'

'That is by custom only,' the bishop replied. 'It can be overruled by an Act in Council, and the proposal is that you first go through an adoption process, following which the council will be ordered to adopt an ordinance that names you as heir. It would, however, first be required that you give each other the kiss of peace in my cathedral, following which you must do homage to Stephen as the current king.'

Henry sat deep in thought, his brow furrowed, while Richard and Robert held their breath. Then he looked up and nodded. 'Tell your master that I will give due and urgent regard to his proposal. You will, however, appreciate that I need to take counsel before considering whether or not to give agreement to it.'

'Naturally,' the bishop replied as he reached for a parchment, which he unfurled and held out for Richard to step forward and accept from him. 'The terms I have just outlined are recorded here. May I hope that we shall meet again in early course?'

'You may,' Henry replied with a curt nod. 'Now, if you would excuse us?'

Once they were alone, Henry swallowed down an entire mug of wine in one gulp, burped, and turned to Richard and Robert. 'Well?' he demanded. 'Where is the trap?'

'We should not necessarily proceed on the assumption that there *is* a trap,' Richard suggested, then felt a spasm of fear as Henry's face reddened.

'The offer we just received was almost exactly that which you predicted,' Henry pointed out suspiciously. 'Have you been meeting with your uncle behind my back?'

'You have my word that I have not,' Richard replied. 'It is merely the case that Stephen and I came up with the same path out of the impasse. Perhaps it is the result of our being related, over which I have no control.'

'And are you by any chance related to an astute lawyer who can ensure that we are not played false by whatever parcel of words Stephen comes up with?' Henry fired back grumpily. 'We are at risk of being outplayed by words instead of force of arms.'

'You are minded to at least consider the proposal?' Robert enquired.

Henry nodded. 'The ultimate prize will be the throne of England, and it may, by this means, be acquired without any further expense. The men at arms we brought with us from Normandy are costing me dearly on a daily basis, and not only do I wish to be in a position to discharge them, but I must soon return to Poitiers for the birth of my firstborn by Eleanor. I also do not wish those peasants in Poitou to become too content with my absence. So yes, I propose that we agree in principle to what is being offered, but demand that it be put in written form, and that we then employ the best lawyers we can find who can search for the hidden traps before we sign.'

This was achieved on the third day, and arrangements were made for the kiss of peace to be exchanged in a week's time inside the ancient cathedral in Winchester. Henry then began making plans for his return home, which he kept as unobtrusive as the circumstances permitted.

IV

Richard was given leave to return to his estate for a few days, ahead of accompanying Henry back across the Channel. As he was in the process of dismounting outside the stable door, he heard the familiar voice welcoming him home, and he turned to hug Agnes to him.

'Don't worry, I'll remove my boots before I go inside,' he assured her.

'When you do, you have a visitor,' she said. 'He's been here for two days, and a fine-looking young man he is, too. Lucy and Amy are likely to come to blows in their competition to ensnare him, so the sooner he leaves the sooner we can enjoy normal table service again.'

Intrigued, Richard strode into the hall, where a young man with flowing black locks was sitting by the empty fireplace. He rose and turned, and Richard smiled as the memories flooded back.

'I have but recently been reunited with one nephew, and now the second one comes looking for me. Was ever an uncle so blessed? Welcome to my estate, William.'

'I wasn't sure if I'd be welcome here,' William replied sheepishly, 'but Alain said that you had expressed a desire to meet with me again. I was rather brusque the last time we met, I'm afraid.'

Richard chuckled. 'I deserved it, expecting you and your brother to be so welcoming when that was only the third time I'd ever put in an appearance. I take it that Alain told you that you would find me here, and that you were indeed working for the chancellor somewhere in Winchester, as he surmised?'

William's face clouded slightly. 'I am indeed, stuck in a dull daily routine copying accounts from one folio to another at the behest of the Dean of York, who's quite the most tedious taskmaster you could imagine. The only bright aspect of my duties is that my master is very dilatory in attesting charters, mainly because he seems to devote much of his time to his ecclesiastical duties. This has resulted in others, including myself, being required to examine them in minute detail before handing them over for attestation. Not only does this leave me free to devote myself to other matters, but it has also resulted in the formation of a firm friendship with another clerk engaged in a similar way. His name is Tom Becket, and he came to the post on the recommendation of Archbishop Theobald, in whose household he formally served. Tom knew my brother Alain from those days, and it was through his good offices that Alain was able to seek me out and advise me that you were asking after me. He also made enquiries as to where your estate was located, and it was conveniently close to Winchester.'

'Do I detect that you are not altogether well suited to your current position?'

'I'm afraid that subtlety is not my strongest virtue,' William confessed with a slightly red countenance, 'and you are correct. I have been educated in the entire common law of England, and a child of eight could be trained to read and assess simple charters for the grant of land from one noble to another, or from some local worthy to the Church. In a word, I am bored to distraction, and am seeking another position in which I could employ all my talents.'

'I would hazard a guess that this visit owes more to that ambition than it does any strong desire to be reunited with your uncle,' Richard smiled, then raised a hand as William opened his mouth in protest. 'No, please don't struggle to deny it. If I can assist you, I will, since I have always looked to your welfare.'

'More so than my parents,' William responded as the two serving maids Lucy and Amy scuttled into the hall where they were seated, giggling and nudging each other as they laid out the trenchers ahead of supper. William turned to grin at each of them in turn and then enquired, 'How do you know that I am not married, and content with my wife?'

Amy almost choked in an effort not to chortle, while Lucy went bright red and ran back towards the kitchen. Amy gave a slight curtsey and ran after her. William leered as she left.

Richard laughed. 'You take after your mother and father, rather than your uncle. They were both pleasing to the eye in their younger years, and you bear a strong resemblance to your father as I remember him in his youth, when he overcame your mother's virtue. I genuinely thank providence that I was not gifted with such attributes, since in my experience it has the potential to lead a man astray. Take the advice of an uncle who has progressed in life by means of other gifts.'

'The same uncle who wooed a wealthy widow in order to acquire this fine estate?' William replied mockingly.

It was Richard's turn to redden. 'I did not need to woo her, since King Stephen all but commanded her to marry me. I don't believe that she has come to regret that decision, and I most certainly have not.'

'That was perhaps as well,' came Agnes's strident voice from close behind him, 'but that does not give you the right to plunge what was once my exclusive estate into chaos by slipping this handsome devil into my household like a fox into a hencoop. Amy and Lucy are almost beyond carrying out even the most basic instructions. Please do not let this man remain for long enough to get them exchanging blows in rivalry for his affections.'

'I promise you that I will not,' Richard chuckled, secretly proud of William. 'In fact, I believe that I shall be taking him away as early as the morrow, in order that he may meet with Duke Henry and de Beaumont.'

William's eyebrows rose in an expression of delight. 'You have a use for me?'

'Indeed I do — or rather, Henry does. As your brother has no doubt already told you, Duke Henry is visiting Winchester, along with his military commander Robert de Beaumont, in the hope of negotiating peace terms with King Stephen. We have been presented with a document that sets out the terms upon which the kiss of peace may be exchanged, but Henry is suspicious, and has asked me to search for a lawyer who can assure him that he is not being swindled out of something important. Your arrival here is, I believe, a good omen, since you are such a lawyer, and you are in search of advancement. Would you be able to fulfil Henry's commission?'

'I won't know until I try, but since I came here hoping for a way out of that dreadful Chancery Chamber, then surely some guardian angel is guiding my footsteps,' William smiled as the maids came in with platters of fish, fowl and fruit, accompanied by a stern-faced Agnes who watched them carefully as they loaded the board, curtsied and bowed out, all without a single giggle or sideways look.

'He's your nephew, you say?' Henry enquired as he pushed the empty platter to one side, having consumed enough for three. 'Better bring him in. Let's see what he can tell us, if anything.'

Richard slipped back out into the corridor, where a nervous William was waiting to be invited into the presence. His first vision of the man from Anjou who might well be his next king was of a red-faced, somewhat overweight, and scruffily dressed man who hardly looked old enough to require a barber for his beard, and who was struggling to extract a piece of meat from between his teeth. Henry reached out to a side table, picked up a parchment roll and threw it towards William, who caught it deftly before finally bowing.

'Tell me if you can find any flaws or traps in that,' Henry commanded him.

William read the document carefully before stating the obvious. 'It appears to bestow the crown of England upon you, following the death of King Stephen.'

'I know that, you fool!' Henry replied curtly with an exasperated look across at Richard. 'What I need to know is what it does *not* say. If, for example, it differs in any important regard from documents of this nature that you are accustomed to drafting or perusing.'

'There is, of course, the matter of the failure to mention heirs, my lord.'

'Of *course* there is,' Henry confirmed grumpily. 'That's the whole point of the document — it gives me the crown while cutting out Stephen's heirs, who might otherwise claim it.'

'I was referring to your own heirs, my lord,' William replied deferentially.

Henry looked up sharply, then across at Richard and Robert in turn. 'What *about* my heirs?'

'Well,' William began, 'I have a lengthy experience of drafting charters for land transfers, and in those it is traditional for the donor to convey not only to the person receiving the grant, but also to their "heirs and successors". This document appears to convey the crown of England to you upon the death of King

Stephen, but despite the very recent death of Eustace, does he not have a remaining son? The young Prince William?'

'Yes,' Henry replied eagerly. 'So what are you telling me, young man?'

'That this document only conveys the crown to you, and not to any heirs you may have. On your death, what is to prevent Stephen's heir claiming that he was intended to get what we lawyers call the "reversion", and commencing fresh hostilities?'

Henry glared at Robert. 'Can that happen? And if so, why did you not warn me of that possibility?'

'As to your second question, I'm not an experienced common lawyer, like our young friend here. As to the first, it would be no different from your claim in right of your mother.'

'So we need to have the terms of the peace treaty amended?' Henry enquired testily.

Robert nodded. 'So it would seem.'

'Can you make the necessary amendment?' Henry asked William.

'Of course, since it merely requires the addition of a few more words. And the person who drafted it on behalf of King Stephen was my own brother.'

'See to it,' Henry instructed him, 'but not until you have shared a mug of wine with me. Then we might discuss your future in my service.'

After William had departed with a smug smile, Richard asked, 'What had you in mind for my nephew — sire?'

Henry preened at the use of the title, then looked at Robert de Beaumont. 'You clearly have little understanding of legal matters, yet I would have you become my Chief Justiciar in due course. Would it not be a wise move to have at your side someone who actually understands the matters over which you would be presiding?'

'Undoubtedly,' Robert conceded.

Henry turned his gaze upon Richard. 'Think you that he would accept such a position?'

'I have no doubt that he would — and gladly,' Richard replied.

Three days later, the ceremony took place under the vaulted ceiling of Winchester Cathedral. Archbishop Theobald read out the terms of what was to be known as the Treaty of Winchester, under which Stephen acknowledged Henry as his adopted son and the heir to England, in return for Henry paying homage to him and promising to return across the Channel without delay. It was further agreed that Stephen's second son William would in due course pay homage to Henry, and renounce his claim to the throne, in return for pledges on Henry's part to honour his titles to the various lands and castles that he currently possessed.

The older son Eustace having died only a month previously, struck down by an unidentified malady that Archbishop Theobald ascribed to the wrath of God following Eustace's plundering of several abbeys in East Anglia, there was no-one other than Prince William who would be likely to contest the transfer of the crown into the Angevin dynasty. His expression was bleak and disapproving as his father and Henry exchanged the kiss of peace under a holy banner held high by two monks from Canterbury, one of whom was William's twin brother Alain.

The new Treaty recognised the right of Henry's heirs to succeed him onto the throne of England, and this was the best outcome that could have been desired by the new heir apparent. He was very drunk several hours later, back in Stockbridge, when he announced slurringly that 'William of Walsingham' would be joining his inner circle as they all journeyed back to Poitiers following the arrival of a breathless messenger with the happy news that Eleanor had borne Henry a son called William.

'Two new Williams in my life,' Henry burped as he swayed gently towards his garderobe, in the belief that he would shortly be vomiting into it. 'God has blessed me twice with saviours of my royal house, and He has called them both William.'

'Do not become too swollen-headed,' Richard whispered to William as they watched Henry's lurching figure leave the hall. 'Your true bloodlines are less elevated, and you do not come direct from God.'

Henry and Eleanor were joyfully reunited, and a banquet was ordered, both to celebrate the birth of a son and heir and to announce his elevation, at the age of three weeks, to the status of Count of Poitiers. The Lady Maude was persuaded out of her self-imposed seclusion at the Priory of Notre Dame du Pré, on the outskirts of Caen, and the planned banquet promised to be the sort of grand affair that continued for several days and left everyone feeling somewhat seedy.

On the morning of the proposed banquet Richard was in the guardhouse, allocating patrol duties for the day, when a man dressed in a tunic bearing the livery of Anjou that was stained with sweat rushed in, almost breathless. 'I bring an urgent message from Duke Henry, sir.'

Richard rose in alarm. 'What has happened? Is the duke in immediate danger?'

'No, sir,' the messenger panted. 'In truth, I am on my way with a small detachment of men to meet the train of the Lady Maude to escort it back to Caen. The banquet is cancelled. I was also commanded to seek you out before I depart, and pass on an order from the duke that you lose no time in saddling up your best men for a royal escort back to England.'

'Has the peace treaty been broken already?'

'No, sir, it is about to be fulfilled as intended. Stephen is dead, and Duke Henry is now King of England.'

V

The coronation inside Westminster Abbey on 19th December 1154 was a glittering affair presided over by the Archbishop of Canterbury, flanked by the remaining bishops of England whose sees had not been allowed to lie vacant by the former King Stephen. Henry proudly wore his ducal robes, to remind the lesser mortals packed inside the cathedral that he had estates across the Channel, and he had even deigned to shave and bathe for the occasion. But it would have irked him to learn that he was not the centre of attention.

This distinction was reserved for Queen Eleanor, crowned alongside Henry and outshining even the clergy in her finery, chosen with skilful taste to emphasise both her height and her natural beauty, while concealing the fact that she was again with child. It was the first sight of her that even the English nobles had been allowed, since the royal couple had, since their landing almost two weeks previously, been all but hidden away in the old Saxon Palace of Bermondsey. This was due to the spiteful vandalising of Westminster Palace by Stephen's old guard supporters following his death, and the realisation that the House of Anjou had finally triumphed over the House of Blois.

If Henry had experienced any doubt regarding the popularity of the new regime, this was dispelled by the cries of '*Vivat Rex*!' that followed the placing on his head of the crown that had once been lowered onto the head of his great-grandfather, the fabled William of Normandy. The triumphal procession back to a hastily restored Westminster Palace was lined with thousands of Londoners calling for Henry's long life, and giving thanks to God that the extended period of warfare was finally at an end, and that the mighty prince had pledged to restore the nation to its former prosperity.

But before he could achieve that, Henry needed to restore law and order, and he wasted no time in appointing a new Chief Justiciar. In fact, he appointed two, since in addition to honouring his promise to award the prestigious position to his loyal Earl of Leicester, Robert de Beaumont, he also felt obliged to install, in a joint office, someone who had actual experience of administering royal justice. His choice was Richard de Lucy, County Justiciar and Sheriff of Essex. The two men were summoned to Henry's Throne Chamber on the morning following the coronation banquet, where a surprisingly alert and seemingly sober Henry outlined what he required of them.

'You are to work harmoniously for the restoration of peace throughout the nation, is that understood?' he demanded sternly as they stood before him, suitably silent. 'There is to be no bickering, no rivalry, and no working behind each other's backs to undermine the authority of the other. The first suggestion of that and the offender will be dismissed from office. To that end, I require your solemn oaths — here and now, before me — so kneel and swear!'

The two men did as required, overawed by the strength and obvious sincerity of the young king. When they were invited to rise and take the seats allocated to them on either side of the recently restored throne seat, Henry lost no time in telling them what he had in mind.

'I have succeeded in wringing reports from those who feared my wrath so greatly that they recently bowed the knee and sought forgiveness for serving the previous usurper. From what I have heard, the nation has become almost ungovernable. Castles have been erected without royal sanction, the revenues have not been flowing into the Treasury as they should, the forest laws remain unenforced to the extent that every peasant in the land is now dining off royal game, and the local barons are conducting their legal affairs as best suits them. This must all be reversed with the minimum of delay — are we agreed on that?'

Both men nodded, and Henry smiled for the first time since they had been admitted to the presence.

'Excellent. I do not expect this all to occur overnight, or even during the next few weeks, but a year from now I wish you to be in a position to report to me that these abuses of power have been suppressed. Since I would imagine that you are eager to lose no time in bringing all this about, you are dismissed.'

With a look of surprise, the two men rose, bowed, and backed out of the Throne Chamber. Once outside they stood briefly in the hallway, looking out through the mullioned window to the courtyard below. It was de Lucy who broke the silence.

'Well, we were certainly left in no doubt as to what our new monarch requires. How would you propose that we set about working this miracle?'

De Beaumont thought for a moment before offering a reply. 'From what I learned in there, I would suggest that yours is the greater knowledge of the workings of our courts at their various levels, which I must confess has always been something of a mystery to me. There is a young man in my service by the name of William Walsingham, the nephew of the Captain of the Royal Guard Sir Richard Chalfont. He has proved himself skilled in the matter of legal drafting, and is eager to progress in the royal service. I propose that you take him into your office, there to learn how our system of justice currently operates and to suggest improvements, while I set about touring the realm and ordering the destruction of those castles to which King Henry made reference. I will also make enquiry of the chancellor as to the cause of the shortfall in royal revenues. By these means, we should be able to report progress within a matter of weeks.'

'Agreed,' de Lucy smiled. 'Send me this young man of whom you spoke without delay.'

William was surprised, but relieved, to be summoned to the ground floor chambers inside Westminster Palace that were allocated to the Chief Justiciar. He'd been bored sitting around his own humble cottage built into the outer wall of the palace yard, the remains of a row that had originally been constructed by the Saxon King Edward to house his most important palace servants. William was not exactly one of those, but he was grateful to his uncle Richard for having secured the accommodation for him. The alternative might have been a room above the ample stable block, or one of the communal chambers below ground level that were occupied by the more menial of kitchen and laundry staff.

William was frustrated at not having heard anything further of the promised lawyer's work under the lofty Robert de Beaumont, and he'd begun to tire of amusing himself with kitchen and scullery maids, all of whom made themselves available to him in the obvious hope of advancement themselves. Because of his superior accommodation, and the fact that he was officially part of de Beaumont's entourage, the maids clearly regarded William as a good marriage prospect, when in fact marriage was the last thing on his mind.

When Richard advised him that he was required to present himself inside the Chief Justiciar's chambers, William was puzzled that the man who ordered his attendance was not de Beaumont, but the man de Lucy who shared office with him. But at least it was a step in the desired direction, and William put a broad smile on his face when he was finally admitted into the narrow room that was de Lucy's personal office chamber.

'You're the young man who knows all about drafting legal documents?' de Lucy asked.

William nodded. 'However, I don't know too much about the court system, except those in which money is collected for the Exchequer on land transfers such as wardship, marriage or *bona vacantia*.'

'That will do to begin with,' de Lucy conceded, 'but you have much to learn if we are to restore the court network to what it should be. I've drawn up this document for you to take away and study, in order to familiarise yourself with how it's supposed to work. It will then be a matter of you, and others, touring the nation in order to report back to me which courts are being regularly convened, and which have fallen into disuse.'

William looked briefly at the large vellum that he was handed. 'That seems straightforward enough, so perhaps I might make a start tomorrow, after I've studied this.'

De Lucy smiled indulgently. 'You cannot even begin to make a start until you know where these various courts are located, so I propose that you begin with my own county of Essex. I have a castle and a surrounding estate at Ongar, which is only a good day's ride from here, and I shall expect you on Saturday of this week. We may then spend a few days inspecting the court system of which I am the sheriff, with a court of my own. You may also familiarise yourself with my household, since I imagine that you will be a frequent visitor in the months to come, as you report back your findings to me.'

William thanked him warmly and bowed out of the chamber. He was back out in the courtyard that lay outside the ground floor suite of chambers when he heard a commanding voice demanding his attention, and turned to see Robert de Beaumont in the doorway that he'd just left by.

'I trust that we've found some useful task for your talents, young man?'

'Indeed,' William confirmed. 'Justiciar de Lucy has set me on a mission to learn which of our courts are still functioning, and which are not. I shall be travelling the length and breadth of the realm for the best part of a year.'

'Excellent,' de Beaumont smiled. 'It may be that our paths will cross, since my allotted task is to traverse the nation pulling down castles that have sprung up without royal permission. I must also attempt to gauge the loss to the Exchequer of dues withheld from the royal purse.'

'That's clearly a Chancery matter,' William reminded him, 'and should you require assistance from someone well familiar with those occasions that should have resulted in a payment, then seek out a young clerk called Tom Becket. He and I worked alongside each other at Winchester, and he is a pleasant enough young man, much given to deep thought and reflection, but also devoted to whatever task he is set.'

'I will, and thank you for the guidance,' de Beaumont replied, then waved his hand in a gesture of farewell as William made his way back to his cottage.

Once there, he poured himself a mug of the wine that had been delivered from the kitchen by his houseboy Bodwyn. He then sat down by the window to take advantage of the clear winter sunlight after stacking more logs on the fire in the alcove to the side.

What he discovered as he read was a confusing, unequal and haphazard collection of forums for the provision of justice and the settlement of disputes. Most lords of the manor had the authority to establish and preside over courts of their own, and issue judgments in matters of local contest. Above them were the sheriffs, who also had courts in which those accused of criminal acts could be brought to trial. Given that the outcomes of such trials included hangings, such courts were obviously of prime importance in securing peace and tranquillity throughout the realm, and suppressing lawlessness.

But the number of recorded sittings of such courts varied alarmingly from one area of the country to another, and it seemed that the further away from London one travelled, the more infrequent were the sittings held by sheriffs. Counties close to the capital such as Surrey, Kent and Essex were in almost permanent sitting, whereas parts of Yorkshire, Lancashire and Cornwall seemed to hold courts irregularly, almost at the whim of the sheriff rather than in response to the crimes that were reported.

But one of the most alarming conclusions that William reached, when he gained access to such records as existed within the Justiciar's Office, was that the *types* of crime dealt with seemed to differ considerably from district to district. For example, either there was no crime of murder recognised in Yorkshire, or the men of the north were more respectful of human life, which was barely credible. Even more alarming was the discovery that there seemed to be no means of bringing to justice the most powerful barons of all. A sheriff had notional jurisdiction over all crimes in his geographical area, but not once could William point to a baron being held accountable for a serious crime such as murder, rape, kidnap or robbery. It seemed as if they lived a charmed life, free of any risk of punishment for those acts of brutality for which they were infamous.

Then there were the Church courts, presided over at their very highest by a local bishop. If a cleric of any description was even accused of a crime — in itself a rare event — it seemed that he could claim the right to be tried in a court convened by his ecclesiastical superior. Even if found guilty, he would receive a merciful punishment, usually consisting of the imposition of penances that rarely exceeded excessive 'counting' of rosary beads, which was something he did in the ordinary course of things anyway.

An element of religious superstition also seemed to have crept into the forms of trial, even in those courts that were not governed by the Church. An appeal to God to reveal the guilt or innocence of the accused person could be made by means of subjecting them to something called the 'ordeal', the outcome of which would be governed, or so it was believed, by the hand of God, regardless of what those who had witnessed the crime had to say on the matter.

All in all, it was a shambles, William concluded — a hotchpotch of a justice system that was flexible to the point of unpredictability, open to bribery or other forms of corruption, and uneven in its effects. If King Henry was serious about implementing a justice system that was effective in maintaining the peace of the realm, and suppressing abuses by the most powerful, then the justiciars had a good deal of difficult work ahead of them.

He lost no time in revealing his findings to de Lucy shortly after his arrival on his first visit to Ongar Castle, and the justiciar nodded sagely.

'There is much truth in what you say, and I am grateful to you for the careful enquiry you have made, but the king will wish to hear more than simply how pathetic is the current system. He will need proposals for the future provision of justice that are workable, and above all inexpensive. This must be your next task, and I wish you the very best of luck.'

VI

There were massive celebrations the following month in Oxford, to which the Court had retreated for the birth of Henry and Eleanor's second child, another son who they called Henry, after his father. Since the firstborn, William, was showing signs of frailty as he entered his second year, and since Henry abhorred any sign of weakness in anyone, most of all those closest to him, he poured all his ambition into the sturdy, squawking bundle that was handed to him by the midwife. By the time Queen Eleanor was back on her feet, the child had been proclaimed throughout the nation as Young Henry, heir apparent to England, Normandy, Anjou, Aquitaine, Poitou and Maine.

It was also time to give some thought to how matters were progressing across the Channel in those possessions that now had a nominated heir. The somewhat uncertain and informal peace that existed between Henry and his arch rival Louis of France would not last forever, given that the no-man's land between them known as the Vexin remained disputed territory. There was also the continued interference of Henry in the governance of Brittany, which he was anxious to add to his territories in order to control the whole of the northern half of the Continent.

But for a brief while the royal court was relaxed, and Richard was relieved that his duties as Captain of the Royal Guard could be delegated to his most trusted second in command, Ralph Bugge, a career soldier who owed his entire advancement to Richard. He demonstrated his gratitude by keeping to himself the fact that his immediate superior was beginning to feel his years, particularly in the soreness of his joints and his shortness of breath when climbing staircases.

Given the relative proximity of Oxford to his estate at Chalfont, the ageing Richard was able to spend increasing periods away from Court in the company of his ailing wife Agnes. She seemed to succumb to every winter chill, and every stiff wind of early spring, resulting in her being increasingly confined to her bed, with roaring fires lit daily and endless supplies of mulled ale and beef stew being carried up the rickety staircase.

Agnes and Richard were regularly joined by William, following his first survey of those matters that Henry had allocated to him.

'So how go your plans to present Henry with a system that will control the powerful barons who hang around his Court with such ingratiating manners?' Richard enquired. 'Henry cannot see it for himself, but they are all a potential threat to his personal safety.'

'I have a scheme in my head,' William replied, 'but I need some diversion before I can complete my plans for a new system of royal justice.'

'I have the perfect opportunity for you,' Richard grinned. 'Henry wishes, in due course, to return to Poitiers, in the hope of lifting Queen Eleanor's spirits after the death of their firstborn, William. I am obliged to accompany him, although his day-to-day safety will rest in the hands of Ralph Bugge. But I would appreciate your company, if only to assist me into my garments every morning, and take my arm as I mount those numerous narrow staircases in the palace. I am becoming an old man who is in need of a nephew to take the place of the son he never had.'

'I have no better plan,' William replied grudgingly. 'Perhaps when there I may find some beautiful and wealthy lady who can supply me with the happiness that my uncle obviously enjoys.'

In the event, their departure was delayed, first of all by the birth of another royal son, Richard, and then by certain arrangements that had to be put in place that Henry regarded as priorities. Since they involved both Robert de Beaumont and Richard de Lucy, the two Chief Justiciars were summoned to the palace at Oxford that seemed to have become Henry's favoured residence when in England, probably due to its proximity to the hunting lodge at Woodstock.

'I shall shortly be departing for my estates across the Channel,' he advised them, 'there to make certain arrangements that will ensure that England remains at peace with Louis of France. Those arrangements may well result in the drafting of a treaty, and to that end I shall require that wise young lawyer of yours, Robert — the one who prevented me from being cheated by Stephen of Blois.'

'You mean William Walsingham?'

'Is that his name? I forget, remembering only his skill. Ensure that he is instructed to travel in your party.'

'I am to accompany you?' Robert enquired, a little taken aback. He wished to give his whole attention to family matters and had almost succeeded in securing his daughter Amicia a position at Court in which she would be trained as one of Queen Eleanor's ladies.

'Naturally, since I wish you to supervise the appointment of justiciars in each of our provinces of Normandy, Anjou, Poitou and Aquitaine. I wish them to be as well governed as England, and I shall not always be there in person to ensure that they are, hence the need for justiciars. I also wish you to be on hand when we meet with Louis of France and his new bride, who is said to be of the House of Castile and possessed of estates that could prove threatening to ours in Poitou.'

'But what of the discharge of my English duties?' Robert asked.

Henry nodded towards Richard de Lucy. 'That is why I appointed you both as justiciars. Richard here will see to the peaceful governance of England while you and I see to the future interests of Normandy and my other estates. And since you are both here at the same time, how far have you each got in assessing the extent of the threat to law and order here in England?'

'Quite far, sire, although what we have discovered is of considerable concern,' de Lucy began. 'My chosen agent in the matter — the same young man who will shortly be taken from me while you employ him abroad — reports that the further north one travels throughout the nation, the less firm is our command of the legal process, and the less reliable are our courts of justice. I have him currently working on a scheme that will centralise all justice in your hands, and I would hope that I can apprise you of it well within the twelvemonth that was allotted. But of course, if you keep Master William overseas for longer than that…'

'Yes, yes, excuse accepted,' Henry replied brusquely. 'But tell me this much at least, even though it be early days. Does this scheme of yours include the courts of the clergy, or will the nation continue to be at the mercy of murdering monks and fornicating bishops?'

'I am not entirely sure, sire,' de Lucy admitted, 'but you might wish to enquire of him yourself, while he is travelling in your train.'

'Yes, I might well,' Henry nodded, then turned to de Beaumont. 'And what of your enquiries, Robert? Does our Treasury continue to be short-changed, and if so, what are you doing about it?'

De Beaumont smirked. 'If those who paid their dues when the law says that they should were to be honest and forthcoming, then you might expect to be in receipt of a further ten thousand pounds annually.'

'And whence come these calculations?' Henry demanded, both intrigued by the amount and horrified by its extent.

Robert gave a slight bow as he reached inside his tunic and extracted several sheets of vellum. 'I have here a list of those instances of which we are aware in which sums should have been paid into the Treasury on account of feudal occasions such as marriage, inheritance, wardship and *bona vacantia*. There were almost certainly more of which we are not aware, and these amounts refer to only the past year. Further diligent enquiry may well reveal three times this amount.'

'You have compiled these lists yourself?' Henry enquired sceptically.

Robert shook his head. 'Indeed not, sire, although they were compiled on my instruction by a most diligent senior clerk within your chancery — one recommended to me by William Walsingham. His name is Thomas Becket, and should you wish to discuss this matter with him further, he is without.'

'Without what?' Henry quipped. 'Certainly not without brains — bring him hither.'

De Beaumont disappeared briefly into the hallway outside, then returned with an earnest and serious-faced man in his middle years, dressed in simple clerical robes and shod only in sandals that scuffed against the rushes as he walked into the

Audience Chamber. He executed a deep bow a few feet from where Henry was seated.

'As the justiciar may already have revealed, I am well pleased with your diligence in identifying these shortfalls in royal revenue, due to malfeasance on the part of those who were due to make payment,' said Henry. 'My next question is how you propose that we recoup what we are due and prevent further withholdings.'

'It is simply a matter of distraining the property of those guilty of malingering, sire,' Becket replied. 'Deprive a man of his favourite mount, or perhaps a stable full of them, or raid his country estate for valuable items of religious art, and they will be happy to pay their dues, particularly if, for example, the sum due is ten pounds and the horse is worth fifty.'

'A cunning notion,' Henry conceded, 'but it would take much management, which in itself would cost, perhaps, more than the value of the sum recovered.'

Becket shrugged. 'Not necessarily, sire. The distraint can be ordered by a local sheriff, or some other judicial officer, whereupon it becomes a simple matter of sending in the local constables, accompanied by a magistrate or sheriff's bailiff. Once word gets out that the methods employed, and the items distrained, are unreasonable in the extreme, then one might confidently expect a distinct improvement in the frequency of voluntary payment without need to have recourse to the courts.'

Henry chuckled, provoking a knowing grin from Becket, then enquired, 'I see by your garb that you are a man of God — how sit such processes with your conscience?'

'"Give what is Caesar's to Caesar",' Becket answered piously, drawing loud laughter from Henry.

'I like your style — and your use of scripture when it suits my purpose. You are ordained?'

'A monk merely, sire,' Becket advised him with a suitably humble expression, 'and that only so as to be able to reside within the monastery at Canterbury when I served Archbishop Theobald.'

'And now you serve Robert of Ghent, Archdeacon of York, in his capacity as chancellor?'

'I did, sire, until his demise. His office is currently vacant, but I have taken it upon myself to preserve a copy of all incoming records and accounts to await his replacement.'

Henry frowned. 'I was not aware of his death, probably because I never required his attendance here. That is perhaps as well, since he seems to have acted in a dilatory manner.'

'In fairness to him, sire, his duties were divided, and he felt obliged to put God first.'

'And you, Thomas? Who do you put first?'

'Whomsoever I serve, sir. At present, yourself.'

Both de Lucy and de Beaumont sensed what was coming, but were reluctant to speak out against it.

'And serve me further you shall, Thomas,' Henry beamed. 'As of today, you are the Chancellor of England.'

A look of pure amazement crossed Becket's face. He stumbled over what he had intended to say in reply, then allowed his mouth to hang open before kneeling like a penitent before the Pope and muttering, 'I shall endeavour always to perform my duties until the last breath shall leave my body, sire.'

The audience came to a close. A still astonished Becket scuttled ahead of the two earls down the hallway as they paused in front of a window that was being spattered by a sudden rain squall.

'Has Henry lost his wits, think you?' de Beaumont asked, but de Lucy shook his head.

'He is merely desperate to have about him men he can trust, which is why you and I were appointed. Let us never forget that.'

Henry's precise purpose in returning to Normandy, once Queen Eleanor had recovered from her latest lying-in, was not disclosed to anyone until they were back in Caen, and meeting around the supper table. It was a hastily assembled company, consisting of those highly placed in the royal estimation.

Henry and Eleanor sat side by side at the head of the table, with her attendant Lady Adele standing behind her in case she required assistance. Down each side, separated by the table itself, as if to prevent them coming to blows, sat two of the most powerful barons on either side of the Channel. Their families had, until recently, been sworn enemies, and the uneasy body language between them as they sat carving from the huge roasts suggested that the recent peace agreement that they had reached could be shattered by an awkward word.

Hugh de Kevilioc, fifth Earl of Chester, had a great deal of family disgrace to live down, and was anxious to prove the ongoing loyalty of the current generation to King Henry. Hugh's father Ranulf, the fourth Earl of Chester, had been enraged by the terms of the peace treaty that King Stephen had negotiated with King David of Scotland, which had included the alienation of most of Cumberland and Lancaster to the Scots — land that Ranulf claimed had rightfully belonged to his family.

Ranulf had responded by throwing in his hand with Maude, the rival claimant to Stephen's throne, to the extent of marrying Maude's niece, the daughter of her greatest ally, her half-brother Robert of Gloucester. Hugh was the offspring of that marriage, but before he was even born his father Ranulf had defected back to Stephen in the hope of retaining his castle at Lincoln and gaining Stephen's assistance in reclaiming lands lost to him in Normandy.

Part of his support for Stephen had involved him bringing three hundred knights to the long drawn-out siege of Wallingford, but despite that his enemies at Court poisoned Stephen's mind against Ranulf, who was imprisoned until he agreed to foreswear all his estates. He feigned agreement, then immediately formed a secret alliance with the young Henry Plantagenet and King David of Scotland to attack York. The planned attack was abandoned, but Ranulf provided a diversion for Henry and his retreating forces by attacking Lincoln, drawing Stephen's men away from any pursuit.

In gratitude, Henry restored to Ranulf his former estates in Leicestershire and Warwickshire, reviving the old family feud between the Earls of Chester and Leicester which was resolved by an elaborate treaty in whose longevity no-one had any faith. Robert de Beaumont now also had the favoured ear of King Henry, given his appointment as joint Chief Justiciar of England. The heir to the Earldom of Chester, Hugh, barely into his teens, was walking on eggshells as he meekly fulfilled his role as chaperone to his older half-sister Adele, whose mother, by dint of her family connections with the House of Anjou, had secured a place for her as one of Queen Eleanor's ladies.

But even in this it seemed that the rivalry between the Earls of Chester and Leicester was destined to continue into the next generation, because, not wishing to lose out, Robert de Beaumont had also now persuaded Eleanor to take into training his daughter Amicia as another potential lady. She was still only six years old, but already impeccably educated in various languages, in addition to being gifted with a melodious singing voice and a devotion to the Scriptures. She promised much on the marriage market, and Robert was hoping that among the high-ranking knights and barons in Normandy, Anjou, Aquitaine or Poitou there would in due course be a suitable offer for her hand, if only by betrothal until she came of age.

At the foot of the table, still wondering why they had been summoned, sat uncle and nephew Sir Richard Chalfont and William Walsingham. Richard was still officially Captain of the Royal Guard, but no-one expected him, in his advancing years, to actually wield a sword in defence of the king. Instead, his role was simply that of organising the daily details of those who would, led as ever by his second in command Ralph Bugge. Richard's continued office, and presence at the supper table, was more in recognition of the role he had played in preserving Henry's mother Maude during the conflict that had resulted in the Treaty of Winchester, and Henry's ultimate accession.

As for William, he had been advised by de Beaumont only that they would be heading to Paris in due course, the stronghold of Louis of France, and that if things went to plan there would be a peace treaty. William's role would be to apply his legal eye to its terms and ensure that there were no serious loopholes that could operate to Henry's disadvantage. He had also been told that any that worked in Henry's favour should not be mentioned. But not even de Beaumont seemed to have any prior information regarding what the terms of the proposed treaty would be. Everyone was hoping that this meeting had been called in order to reveal them, and their curiosity was about to be satisfied.

Henry gave a polite burp, which was as good as a herald blowing a fanfare, since everyone recognised it as a sign that the king was about to speak.

'Most of you will be aware,' he announced, 'that Louis of France married into the House of Castile last year. What may *not* yet have become common knowledge is that his young bride Constance recently gave birth to a daughter, Margaret. She is, of course, the third daughter born to him, the first two being the offspring of dear Eleanor here. A new Princess of France deserves a suitable bridegroom drawn from the best royal house in Christendom, which is of course mine. I now have two sons, one of whom — the young Henry — is now approaching three years of age. What better way to unite the royal houses of England and France in a perpetual peace?'

In the polite silence that followed, a sharp intake of breath could be heard from Eleanor, whose face reddened with displeasure. 'You intend to marry off our second son to the mewling spawn of that idiot?' she complained. 'You might at least have consulted me first!'

'I am the King of England,' Henry retorted hotly, 'and *I* alone decide how its affairs should be conducted. Why should that not include a most valuable match for my son?'

'Because he's *our* son,' Eleanor replied sharply as she rose from her seat and swept from the hall, Adele following closely behind her. She paused by the door to the withdrawing chamber and called back, 'I did not incur the hazards of childbirth simply in order to provide human pieces for your chessboard!'

As she disappeared from sight, everyone handled the embarrassment in their own way. Mainly it consisted of staring down at the board, and pretending to be so absorbed in eating that it was not appropriate to raise one's eyes above it.

When everyone had eaten more than sufficient, Henry advised the remainder of the company that they might withdraw, while signalling that he wished William to remain. Once they were alone, he revealed what was on his mind.

'De Lucy advises me that you have some great scheme in your head for the improvement of the English courts.'

'Indeed, sire, although I have yet to commit it to writing.'

'That is of no concern to me at this stage — simply tell me in broad detail what you have in mind.'

William cleared his throat and began. 'As I have already reported to the justiciars, too much freedom is afforded to those who administer the law notionally in your name. I say "notionally" because, I am sad to relate, many of those who have secured office have proceeded to act solely in their own interests, and with woeful partiality. What is needed is a centralised system of justice with yourself at the very top.'

'Am I not already the fount of all justice?' Henry argued with a frown.

'You are indeed, but only in respect of those matters that are referred directly to your Council. There are countless other matters at a lower level of which you remain unaware, and over which, in reality, you have no control.'

'So what is your solution, pray?'

'A system that begins at the top, and sweeps down across the entire nation like heavy and consistent rain, sire. You are at the very pinnacle of this system, and yours is the law that is enforced. But at present it is shamed and lessened by petty barons and dishonest villains who claim to enforce the law, when in fact they subvert it to their own ends. Those who administer the royal justice should themselves be royal justices.'

Henry's brow furrowed with the effort of comprehending such a scheme, so William explained further.

'The royal court, and the justice it administers, will be carried throughout the land by a new breed of men appointed by you — when they sit in their courts, they are, in effect, you in person. This way, "the king" is dispensing the law directly from his own hand, through the hands of those who are appointed. We might even call them "justices", to enforce the point.'

Henry looked troubled. 'Would it be wise to grant so much power to one man? Would they not come to consider themselves as powerful and important as myself?'

'There would be that risk, sire, I concede. You must therefore choose such men with the greatest of care, and ensure that they are ultimately answerable to you. But the great advantage would be that the same law would be enforced throughout the realm, equally among all men.'

'And what of the clergy? You are aware that they claim the right to hold their own courts, and thereby shield their own from the consequences of their law-breaking?'

'Indeed, but under my system all men will be answerable to your law, regardless of their rank or calling, from the highest born noble to the humblest parish priest.'

'Have you discussed this notion with the chancellor?'

'Why should I have done, sire? His is not the responsibility of enforcing your law in the common courts of the realm. And of course there is at present no chancellor.'

'There is now — a man called Thomas Becket, who I appointed to the office shortly before we left England. He was previously in the employ of the chancellor.'

William smiled. 'By happy coincidence he is well known to my brother Alain, who served with him in Canterbury. Do you wish me to consult him regarding my proposals?'

'It would be best, and without delay, since his is the responsibility of enforcing those laws that bring revenue into the Exchequer. But you will perforce need to wait until we return to England.'

'Should I not perhaps do so now, in view of your suggestion that I meet with Becket without delay?'

'No, since I require you at my side when we meet with Louis of France. I do not trust him. Now, I am long overdue a meeting with my garderobe. We shall discuss your proposal when we have another opportunity; for the time being, prepare to journey to Paris.'

VII

Simon, Lord of Evreux and Montfort-l'Amaury, rode out to meet Henry and his entourage as they approached his manor house at Evreux. He reined in his mount a few yards from Henry's, dismounted and gave a flourishing bow.

'Welcome to my estate,' he greeted them.

Henry gave him a warm smile in return. 'I hope that we will not inconvenience you in any way by imposing such a large number upon your household,' he said with just a hint of disparagement.

Simon inclined his head in a polite gesture of humility. 'Far from it. I only hope that it is not too humble an abode for the King of England, since my master Louis bid me make you as welcome and comfortable as befits a monarch. He eagerly anticipates your meeting.'

'As do I,' Henry replied, then turned to indicate the litter in the centre of the progress. 'Perhaps if suitable chambers have been prepared for Queen Eleanor and her attendant lady, they might be escorted inside to rest. I may then introduce the rest of my party.'

This was the signal for Richard to dismount from his courser and assist Eleanor from her litter. He then gently walked her the remaining few yards to the manor house door, where she was received by Simon's mother Agnes and escorted inside with suitable bows and smiles. This left her accompanying lady Adele still seated on the palfrey that she had ridden all the way from Caen alongside her mistress's litter. William, who had been riding alongside his uncle Richard for the entire four days, dismounted as usual, and stood beside Adele's horse as she slid from her side saddle into his supporting arms. As she did so, she hugged him tighter than was necessary and whispered, 'I shall miss these few moments of intimacy. Perhaps we might walk together through these beautiful grounds after supper.'

William blushed and hoped that his unaccustomed nervousness in the presence of a real lady was not obvious. Fumbling for words, he replied, 'I would like that,' before allowing her to take his arm in the progress to the manor doorway.

'Why are you really here, and who are all these nobles who surround your king?' Simon enquired as casually as he could of Richard.

Richard nodded towards the two men walking up from the stables, where they had given strict instructions to the grooms regarding the handling of their horses. 'The older of the two, by a good many years, is Robert de Beaumont, Earl of Leicester and Justiciar of England. The younger man is Hugh, heir to the Chester estates, and de Beaumont's former enemy. At least, the two houses have been at odds for many years, but an uneasy peace seems to have been negotiated. The delightful young lady who accompanies Queen Eleanor is Adele, Hugh's illegitimate older sister. Hugh himself is still a boy, as you can see, whereas de Beaumont is well into his middle years.'

'Has he any offspring?'

'Several. From memory, there are two sons and two daughters, one of whom — the youngest — is back at Caen, where she is being educated in those matters she requires to learn in order to become a queen's lady.'

'So she is young?'

'Very — only around seven or eight years of age, from what I have seen of her.'

'Her name?'

'Amicia — why your special interest in her?'

'Later. Let us go inside and join the rest of the company ahead of supper.'

'What was that all about?' William asked Richard as he hung back near the doorway to let him catch up.

'I'm not sure,' Richard replied, 'but unless I misjudge our host, I believe that we may be called upon to organise a betrothal ere we leave here for Paris.'

'Our host already has a wife, although we have yet to meet her,' William reminded him.

'Yes, but he has a son, also called Simon in the family tradition. He would be of marriageable age by now, and I suspect that his father wishes to strengthen his English connections ahead of the reuniting of the English and French crowns by way of a betrothal. No doubt he will require someone to grease the wheels in that direction.'

The atmosphere around the supper table was guarded and nervous, largely because the English visitors were aware that their host was one of King Louis' most trusted and respected nobles, but also partly because of the pinch-faced countenance of Queen Eleanor. William put this down to her unease at being back in the territory of which she was once queen, and which she had left in virtual disgrace. He also suspected that she had not yet recovered her equanimity after learning that the reason for their journey was the proposed betrothal of her oldest surviving son, the Young Henry, to a daughter of her former husband. He had guessed correctly, because Eleanor knew Louis to be weak, indecisive, and too given over to excessive religious observances. If his daughter Margaret had inherited those traits, then poor Henry would be condemned to a cold marriage.

'It is of considerable relief to me that England and France are still at peace,' Simon observed as he beckoned to the servers for the next courses to be brought to the board, 'given my difficult situation.'

'I was not aware that your loyalties were divided,' said de Beaumont. 'You are King Louis' man, are you not?'

The air between them cooled as Simon replied, 'True it is that I am sworn to Louis in respect of both my estates, but until the former King Henry gave this estate away, I was of course also sworn to him.'

'At least, by that process, my grandfather relieved you of the pain of divided loyalties,' Henry said sharply, almost in rebuke for Simon's insolence. 'But now that you are completely Louis' man, how do you believe that he will receive our delegation?'

'That will depend upon its purpose,' Simon said evasively.

'No doubt you have been charged with the duty of finding out why we really journey to Paris, and it is no great secret,' said Henry. 'Any one of my nobles could have told you, had you asked. But I will relieve you of that burden. We are here to propose the betrothal of my heir apparent Henry to Louis' daughter Margaret.'

'Why should Henry be regarded as the heir apparent?' Eleanor asked coldly. 'He has a brother, Richard, does he not?'

'Henry is the first-born,' Henry replied. 'They may have done things differently during your youth in Poitou, but in England it is the older son who inherits.'

'So Richard will get nothing?' Eleanor demanded.

Henry shook his head. 'Did I say that, woman? Henry will get England and Normandy, and Richard can have Aquitaine and Poitou for all I care. I also have an eye on Brittany, so he can have that as well.'

'I have eaten enough,' Eleanor announced. She rose, threw her napkin down, turned and swept out of the hall with Adele close behind her.

It fell horribly silent, and those around the board only drew breath again when Henry smiled, muttered, 'Women!' and went back to carving from the roast pig.

An hour later, Richard was being escorted round the gardens by Simon, who broached a new topic.

'There would seem to be some tension between your master and mistress.'

'Only when the topic is their sons,' Richard assured him. 'In all other matters they would seem to be compatible, and Chester's sister Adele believes that Eleanor may be with child yet again, so clearly all is well in the bedchamber. It's a pity that she has not yet borne any daughters, then Henry might have other bargaining counters for his territorial ambitions.'

'On the subject of important betrothals,' Simon replied after looking carefully behind him and lowering his voice, 'I grow increasingly concerned regarding my isolation here in the Vexin. While Evreux was under the suzerainty of England, I always felt that I had an ally against Louis, should he turn his mean moods against me. However, now I am totally committed to him, though I perceive Henry to be the stronger of the two. Certainly he has greater territories, and therefore more barons on whom he can call in time of war. We would be open to attack as French possessions as matters stand, and I wish to marry off my son Simon in such a way that we can rely on English family connections should France fall to England.'

'What had you in mind — a noble English bride for young Simon?'

'Precisely. We spoke earlier of the young daughter of the Earl of Leicester — "Amicia", is that her name?'

'Indeed it is, but she is still a mere child,' Richard reminded him.

'I am thinking only of a betrothal at this stage, not a marriage. Would de Beaumont be agreeable to such a match, think you?'

'Whether he is or not, it will require King Henry's formal assent,' Richard advised. 'Do you wish me to make subtle enquiry of de Beaumont?'

'If you would be so obliging. And if my eyes do not deceive me, it would seem to be the season for courtly romance. Is that not the young Earl of Chester walking with my daughter Bertrande? And who are the other two? I think I recognise Queen Eleanor's lady, but who is the tall handsome gallant walking alongside her who reminds me so much of you?'

'He is my nephew,' Richard smiled fondly as he followed Simon's gaze. 'He is a lawyer, and advises King Henry. He is one of twins.'

'And the other one?'

'Still in England in holy orders, working for the Archbishop of Canterbury.'

'Neither of them have followed in the family tradition, then?' Simon observed astutely. 'By your bearing, and the manner in which you follow King Henry like a faithful spaniel, you are a man at arms?'

'I am still his Captain of the Royal Guard, despite my advancing years.'

'Loyalty has its rewards,' Simon nodded. 'It is simply a matter of who to bestow it upon.'

The gardens had indeed become the chosen location for several sedate walks after the heavy supper. William had honoured his earlier half-hearted promise to Adele to accompany her after she waited for him in the hallway once the company rose from the supper table. They were now arm in arm, strolling between two rows of rose bushes that were well past their best, so William assumed that the pleasant perfume was coming from the young lady beside him.

'Will your mistress not miss you?' he asked.

Adele shook her head. 'She has retired for the night, and never requires me once she is asleep. This means that I am left to my own devices in my adjoining chamber, and can spend my time as I wish.'

William was familiar with suggestive comments of this nature, and had regularly pursued them during his many conquests of female domestic staff seeking to ensnare a husband. He doubted, however, that Adele was thus motivated, so opted not to pick up on the allusion. 'The queen seemed to be in an ill humour over supper.'

'She does not wish to be here, given that she was once unhappily married to the king that you are destined to visit. But you will do so without her — and therefore without me — because she refuses to journey any further towards Paris, which brings back such unhappy memories for her. We must therefore make the best of the little time that we have.'

'To what end, precisely?' William asked.

Adele stopped suddenly, pulled firmly on his arm so as to bring them face to face, then kissed him firmly on the lips. 'Whatever you wish, William. I know that you are no virgin, because palace tittle-tattle is full of tales of your prowess as a lover. I have yet to be bedded, and would wish it to be at the hands of someone who knows what they are about. My brother Hugh makes a poor chaperone, so perhaps we might take advantage of my mistress being a heavy sleeper.'

Although fully aroused by such forward talk from a lady not yet twenty years of age who nevertheless had the body of a mature woman, something in the back of William's mind urged caution. She was the half-sister of one of the most powerful barons in England, and one who was an intense rival of his own master de Beaumont. She might well be laying a trap for him, or at the very least hoping to seduce him so as to have a reliable source of information regarding the Earl of Leicester's intentions and actions. To William, she was not so beautiful that she was worth the risk. Very attractive, certainly, with thick tresses of light auburn hair and deep blue eyes, but he could have a woman like her any time he cared to pay serious attention to a servant in the kitchen.

'Is your mistress a heavy sleeper?' he asked, hoping to change the subject while still appearing to be interested in a tryst in her bedchamber.

Adele shrugged. 'That rather depends upon the state of her digestion. You will have noted that of late she has been eating sparingly, as she always does when she is with child. Whatever may be their disagreements regarding the children they have, that doesn't stop her and King Henry coupling to acquire more.'

'So when will this one be due?'

'Who can tell? These matters are not easily calculated, but my guess would be sometime late next year, perhaps in the early autumn.'

Searching for another topic of conversation, William looked behind him, and saw Hugh of Chester walking closely beside a fair-haired young woman of approximately Adele's age. 'Who's that walking with your brother Hugh?' he asked.

'I wish you were as eager as he appears to be. During supper, he was eyeing her as if she were one of the dishes on the board. Her name is Bertrande, and she is a daughter of our host. I made her acquaintance when seeking extra bed linen for my mistress.'

'So you will be remaining here while we journey on to Paris?' They came to the end of the long rose walk, and turned back so that they were walking towards Hugh and Bertrande.

Adele nodded and pulled William closer to her, so that their hips moved in unison as they walked. 'We will, but I'll keep it warm for you if you promise to be more affectionate on your return.'

A further hour into the evening, as they all returned to the manor house after their walks, William was somewhat surprised to hear a knock on his chamber door. It was not, as he feared, Adele with more lascivious suggestions, but Robert de Beaumont, who was clearly hazarding a pretence of enquiring as to William's preparedness for the meeting in Paris. When it became obvious that this had merely been an excuse, and that William had not been fooled by it, de Beaumont came to the point.

'The young lady you were walking with this evening — you realise the risk you were taking?'

William grinned. 'The only risk of which I was aware was that of being hauled off for a wild encounter in her bedchamber.'

'As I suspected,' Robert muttered.

William raised his eyebrows. 'I am not the first, you mean?'

'As to that, I have no knowledge,' Robert replied, 'but I would not put it past that serpent Chester to have set her to ensnare you so as to acquire access to my innermost thoughts.'

'Little risk of that. You have never, so far as I am aware, disclosed a single one of your innermost thoughts to me.'

'Which makes me an accomplished diplomat,' Robert smiled. 'But my warning is more general than that. Beware of becoming too closely aligned with the Chester family — they are as slimy and unpredictable as a sack full of lampreys.'

'I am aware that your two families have long since been at odds, but why should it concern you should I bed one of the daughters of Chester?'

'An illegitimate daughter, remember,' Robert cautioned him. 'She would take no part of any inheritance — that seems destined to go to her idiot brother Hugh.'

'My grandmother was an illegitimate daughter of the House of Blois,' William told him, 'but that did not prevent my uncle benefitting royally from being the nephew of the late King Stephen.'

'In these uncertain times, marriages must be made with the greatest of care,' Robert replied gloomily, 'else one's loyalties become suspect. King Henry clearly seeks to grow closer to King Louis by marrying off their offspring, which is why we are here. And now he wishes me to strengthen the bonds between the nations by offering my little Amicia to the young heir of the House of de Montfort.'

William's eyebrows rose again.

Robert nodded. 'Simon suggested the match to Henry, who was so delighted with it that he will brook no refusal from me. The poor child has yet to see her tenth birthday, so it will be a betrothal only at this stage. Hopefully when the time arrives for it to be consummated we shall once again be at war with France, and the de Montforts will once more be our sworn enemies.'

'I noticed the attention that Hugh of Chester was bestowing upon young Bertrande,' William replied, 'so perhaps in due course there will be two noble English houses that have reasons to look favourably on a prominent French estate.'

'Would that life was much simpler,' Robert muttered as he turned to leave. 'I can only hope that something untoward occurs while we are in Paris that thwarts King Henry's ambition to acquire a French daughter-in-law. I rely on your discretion not to mention that to Henry himself.'

'I know where my best interests lie,' William replied. 'And, by way of further reassurance, they do not lie in a bed alongside one of Queen Eleanor's ladies.'

VIII

The English visitors were relieved to learn that this time, instead of the malodorous Palais de la Cité overlooking the oozing cesspit of the Seine, they were to be received by King Louis in the Palace of Fontainebleau, the newly extended and luxurious former hunting lodge a day's ride south-east of Paris, and more easily accessible from the Vexin.

They had opted to spend the previous night in the comfort of the de Montfort estate of Montfort-l'Amaury, from which it was a pleasant trot across verdant countryside in order to reach Fontainebleau well ahead of the banquet that they anticipated with considerable relish. Louis' famed collection of cooks, unusually, were almost all male, and regarded their skills as a science passed on from father to son.

However, they quickly realised that they were destined to wait, and perhaps sing, for their suppers, when the double doors to the gilded hall were pushed open by richly liveried attendants. Two heralds blew a fanfare as they walked down a long blue carpet towards the thrones, on which sat King Louis and his new queen, Constance of Castile. Their daughter Margaret was now just under a year old, and the ostensible reason for their visit.

Henry did not deign to bow the knee, instead executing a bow from the waist, which evoked a low chuckle from Louis.

'You are fortunate to still be of an age when you can do that,' he smiled at Henry, 'although I see that you bring sufficient in your train to assist you, should you be found wanting. Which reminds me — how fares your queen?'

This could have been considered a blatant insult, implying as it did that Henry might also require assistance in the bedchamber. Richard flexed his sword arm in anticipation while keeping it well away from the hilt, bearing in mind the last time he had caused offence at the French court with a similar gesture.

Henry simply replied, 'She is in excellent health, Your Majesty, and is once again *enceinte*. Perhaps yet another boy?'

Since Eleanor had borne Louis only girls, this could be regarded as a return of the insult, and the honours were now even. Either it could continue in this vein for the remainder of the hour that remained before supper, or they could get down to business. Louis elected for the latter.

'It is the matter of one of your sons that brings you here, is it not, *Henri*? I have heard that your older son is in need of a bride.'

'Indeed,' Henry confirmed, 'and it occurred to me that a lasting and loving peace might be assured between our two nations were my son Henry to become betrothed to your daughter Margaret. Henry is now approaching three years of age, and the difference in ages will seem as nought once they are older, and the marriage itself is celebrated.'

'Your legs must be tired after what, for you, must have been a long journey,' Louis observed sardonically, 'so please take this seat next to me while we discuss possible terms.'

'I would happily dance a jig with your young bride,' Henry replied with a smirk, 'but would be equally content to sit and consider a possible dowry.'

This time the veiled insult verged on offensive, and the Earls of Chester and Leicester both winced with embarrassment. However, Louis merely chuckled and indicated the seat next to his on the opposite side to where Queen Constance sat smiling at the prospect of dancing with someone more her own age.

'I remind you that possession of the lands that lie between our two time-honoured borders has long been a thorn in our relationship,' Louis remarked, 'so I would propose that Margaret's dowry take the form of the Vexin.'

A slow smile crossed Simon de Montfort's face as he contemplated the prospect of his Evreux estate passing back under Henry's suzerainty, but knew enough about political bargaining not to regard the matter as settled. He could also see a slight frown on the face of the young William Walsingham, who had been included in the visiting party in order to guard Henry against any trickery, so he straightened his face and adopted the sort of expression he maintained during card games.

'You require nothing from me?' Henry asked.

Louis shook his head. 'Merely a promise that one day you will get around to swearing fealty to me for all your French possessions.'

'I would be only too happy to do so,' Henry said enigmatically, 'were they in fact French in the first place. Normandy is mine in clear line of descent from the original Duke William, Aquitaine and Poitou became mine upon my marriage, and as for Maine, well, that has long since been claimed by the House of Blois, and we dispute even that.'

Louis chuckled yet again. 'They do not speak falsely when they describe you as a hard man with whom to strike a bargain, Henry. But even if your legs be not tired, your stomach must be rumbling, given its obvious capacity for fine food. Let us withdraw for an hour, then reassemble for the banquet that I have commissioned in your honour.'

'King Henry wishes to speak with you urgently,' Richard advised William just as he was changing from his riding attire into something more courtly. William finished getting ready and walked swiftly down the hallway to the royal guest apartments, where Henry was already dressed for the banquet and looking impatient.

'There you are,' he said in a tone of implied criticism. 'Now, earn your keep — what think you of the offer of the Vexin as a dowry for Princess Margaret?'

William frowned. 'I have only two reservations, sire. The first is that by handing back the Vexin as a marriage dowry for his infant daughter, King Louis is by implication claiming that it is his to gift, whereas you and he have long since been at odds on that issue. There is also the tactical point that wherever might be the border between England and France, it will always be a potential target for either side in any conflict.'

'Your second point is a valid one,' Henry conceded, 'but with the Vexin under English control, we are much closer to Paris within our own territory. We also regain Evreux, which as you will recall is a fine estate, but more to the point its reversion to England will once again confront the powerful de Montforts with divided loyalties. If they can be persuaded to side with England, then we also acquire the advantageous use of Montfort-l'Amaury, which is well within the Île-de-France. Compared with such a strategic advantage, the loss of face regarding whether or not Louis may currently lay claim to the Vexin pales into insignificance. But I thank you for your diligence in pointing out the notional flaw in what is being proposed; your able brain is a distinct advantage to me, and it is high time that I awarded you with an estate.'

'You are too generous, sire,' William murmured.

Henry shook his head. 'I have not yet disclosed the full extent of what I propose.'

William was unsure how to respond, so kept his silence as Henry explained.

'I remain suspicious of the loyalty of the Chester family, given their history of transferring their substantial military might from one cause to another. I therefore wish to place my own man within their estates — one who can warn me of the slightest risk of further treachery from them.'

'Young Earl Hugh is hardly of an age at which he is likely to plot against your throne,' William objected.

Henry raised his hand for silence. 'He will be less inclined to consider treasonous affiliations if he knows that you are watching his every move. I therefore propose to grant to you the manor of Repton, which lies at the southern extreme of the Chester estates, with the Earl of Leicester's lands to the south. Hugh of Chester will rely upon your loyalty at all times, to preserve his southern boundaries, while de Beaumont will not cease in his efforts to get you to yield the estate to him. This way, I get to the keep the balance of power between them, because your first loyalty will be to me.'

'It's a great honour, sire, and reflects the generosity for which you are renowned, but will Earl Hugh not be resentful? Indeed, will he not argue that the estate is not yours to give?'

'No, because *he* will be granting it to you, in return for a favour from me.'

'May I be permitted to know what that is, sire, since it would seem to be the ultimate source of my improvement in fortune?'

'I have given my consent to his marriage to Bertrande of Evreux, which also has the consent of her father Simon, since I have, at the same time, allowed the younger Simon's marriage to Amicia de Beaumont. Just think of the advantage to

England, having two of its most powerful houses joined in matrimony to the family of Louis' most respected knight!'

'Have either of the ladies given *their* consent?' William enquired, adding, 'As I understand it, Amicia is a mere girl.'

'Why should their consent come into it?' Henry asked. 'If it comes to that, you have not yet indicated a willingness, let alone a desire, to wed Adele of Chester, yet you will be doing so.'

William's jaw dropped in amazement. 'She is indeed quite comely, and she has intimated that she finds me attractive, but even so, we have not yet exchanged any promises.'

'But you will, once we return to Evreux, where there will be three betrothal ceremonies, including yours.'

William was appalled at the suggestion that he had no control over his choice of a bride. 'Why *should* I go along with this?'

'Because the estate of Repton is Adele's dowry.'

'And if I refuse?'

'You would disobey your king?'

'Not on any matter pertaining to the welfare of the realm, certainly. But I had rather hoped to be the master of my own destiny.'

'Either you accept this estate, and the bride that goes with it,' Henry advised him ominously, 'or I shall forever block any further attempt on your part to become ennobled. I did not perhaps mention that with the estate I have decided to create an earldom. You may either become the Earl of Repton now, or forever remain simply William Walsingham.'

'I will need to consult my uncle,' William protested in a last despairing effort.

Henry burst out laughing. 'Richard has already given his consent! In fact, he further advises me that you will be honouring a family tradition. He obtained the estate of Chalfont through his marriage to the dowager countess, just as you will acquire the Earldom of Repton by marrying a queen's lady, who — if it is any consolation — has been pursued by several nobles already.'

'I wonder if she was ever caught,' William sneered.

Henry chuckled. 'If she was, then she will be all the more experienced between the sheets. And from what I have learned of your behaviour, she will not be marrying someone who doesn't know what he's doing.'

Once they returned to Evreux, Henry gave orders for a banquet to celebrate the three betrothals. Of the three couples in question, only two had a bride in attendance, since little Lady Amicia was back in Caen, no doubt studying her Latin, Greek, music and catechism under a tutor. De Beaumont therefore stood in for his daughter, ranged incongruously alongside the teenage Simon de Montfort, while on one side of them stood Simon's daughter Bertrande and a very nervous Hugh of Chester. On the other side Adele de Kevilioc, illegitimate half-sister of Hugh, clung to William's hand as if she were controlling her mount. Their palms were already sweaty as William attempted to extract his, incurring a hiss from Adele. 'You will not escape so easily,' she warned.

Much later that evening, a knock on William's door proved not to be a return visit from de Beaumont, but instead a very eager Adele. She slid round the door and rushed across the chamber to where William was lying naked between the sheets. Without any preamble, Adele unhooked her gown and dropped it to the floor, revealing a body that was even more enticing than William had anticipated. Ten minutes later, he had consoled himself that there were other advantages to be had from being Earl of Repton, quite apart from the title.

The major event that year proved to be the birth of a third royal son for whom provision would need to be made in due course. He was named Geoffrey, and like his older brother Richard he was born without any great difficulty in the lying-in chamber designated for Eleanor in Woodstock Palace. After the ritual cleansing with vinegar and smoking pine needles, the chamber was left exactly as it was, in the confident expectation that this would not be the last royal birth for which it would be required.

William and Adele made their first visit to the Repton estate a month after their return to England in Henry's party. It was nestled in the southernmost foothills of Derbyshire, close to the Staffordshire border, and enjoyed lush acreage in the flood plain of the meandering River Trent. It had an ancient church and a small village that housed most of the labourers on what, to judge by the annual accounts that the steward was proud to display to his new master, was a very wealthy and productive estate. It was also Adele's first visit to the estate that had been the dowry carved from the legacy that her younger, but legitimate, brother, had been left on their father's recent death, and which he had been only too happy to part with in order to obtain Henry's consent to his betrothal to Bertrande of Evreux.

Once Adele had gained access to William's bed she proved reluctant to vacate it, and William was hardly disposed to reject her nightly arrivals in his chamber. Such was the delight with which they became accustomed to each other's bodies that several months after their return to court, Adele sought Queen Eleanor's consent to withdraw temporarily from her service in order to deal with her burgeoning stomach. She was due to give birth around Christmas time. She and William opted to remain at Oxford, where the Queen graciously permitted Adele to make use of the midwife and attending physician who had safely delivered her own four boys, three of whom were still alive. The management of the Repton estate — not something to which either of its earl and countess gave any personal attention anyway — was left in the capable hands of its steward Matthew Derby.

As for King Henry, he turned his attention back across the Channel almost as soon as the latest in his brood, Geoffrey, was born. He now had three sons for whom to provide an inheritance, and in his mind England and Normandy were already consigned to Young Henry, while Richard would be left Aquitaine and Poitou. Geoffrey required a legacy that would not be contested by either of his older brothers, and the civil war that had erupted in Brittany following the death of its Duke, Conan III, had created the perfect opportunity for Henry to add to his estates the large north-western expanse of northern Europe that was independent of France. It possessed the strategically important seaport of Saint-Malo to the west of Normandy, through which men at arms might be ferried across from England to defend Henry's existing possessions further south and east.

Henry had for some time claimed the overlordship of Brittany through descent from his grandfather Henry I of England, to whom the lords of Brittany had done homage. With no effective resistance from anyone, not even Louis of France, Henry annexed Brittany, declared his eight-month-old son Geoffrey to be its new count, and defied anyone to assert otherwise.

When no-one did, Henry grew bolder, and all but overreached himself in a new territorial enterprise that was to have implications for the newly elevated Earl William of Retford. This time the target was Toulouse, a town in the south of France that was notionally within Aquitaine, and gave access to the Mediterranean down the Garonne River. It was so far distant from Paris that the Capetian monarchs had never laid claim to it, and its counts had been allowed a degree of independence that encouraged them to regard themselves as monarchs of all they surveyed.

The current Count was Raymond V, a distant relation of the Raymond who had become King of Antioch during the Second Crusade and the uncle with whom Queen Eleanor was rumoured to have had an affair. But his claim was not the strongest in theory, and was even weaker in practice, given the rival claim of Raymond Berenguer of Barcelona that for some reason Queen Eleanor persuaded Henry to support. This raised an immediate prospect of warfare with Louis of France, who had sought to strengthen his alliances to the south of the Île-de-France by marrying his sister Constance to Count Raymond. When Henry marched his forces south towards Toulouse, he learned that Louis was visiting his brother-in-law. Rather than attacking Louis directly, he employed the men at arms he'd brought with him in ravaging and plundering the surrounding countryside. He also sent a clear message to Raymond regarding who really ruled this part of Aquitaine by occupying the town and castle of Quercy. But his almost hollow victory resulted in the loss of a trusted confidant and friend.

As the English men at arms swarmed the walls of Quercy, they came under a hail of missiles hurled by the defenders on their tops. Henry had been in the vanguard of his troops, despite the urgent advice of his Captain of the Royal Guard Sir Richard Chalfont, who had insisted that he move to the rear, in order to watch from a safe distance. But he'd been so engrossed in escorting Henry out of danger by the bridle of his horse that he'd failed to advise his second in command Ralph Bugge of their tactical withdrawal.

Ralph was still in the thick of things, and having left two of his men with orders that King Henry was not to be allowed to venture anywhere, Richard kicked his courser to life and headed back under the walls of Quercy. He'd been in the process of yelling in Ralph's ear that he was to fall back immediately when a lump of rock hit the top of his bare head after he'd briefly removed his battle helm in order to communicate with his colleague. Blood spurted immediately through Richard's thinning, grey hair. A massive crack appeared in his skull and he fell to the ground, lifeless. A horrified Ralph risked everything to dismount and haul Richard's inert form across the saddle of his own horse, then led it to the rear of the English ranks.

Richard never regained consciousness, and Henry was left counting the cost of his vainglorious display of armed force against a community that was technically his to rule in the first place. The broader community of Aquitaine grew even more suspicious and resentful of him, and he had lost an old friend and a loyal adviser.

William, meanwhile, had lost an uncle, and the only member of his family who had ever enquired as to his welfare, along with that of his twin brother Alain, while they had been living the lives of virtual orphans in the care of the Church. He mourned the loss as one would the death of a favourite teacher or a popular parish priest. In any case he was reminded, a month later, of the great circle of life when Adele gave birth to their son, christened Hugh by Archbishop of Canterbury Theobald of Bec three days after he had blessed their union in order to ensure the child's legitimacy in the eyes of God.

The archbishop had been visiting the Court at Oxford, as commanded by King Henry. Theobald had been in poor health for some time, and was relying increasingly on the attendance of one of the more dedicated monks from the monastery attached to his cathedral. This monk's chosen ecclesiastical name was Brother Benedict, but he had been born Alain Walsingham — William's twin brother. He rejoiced in the birth of his nephew, but both he and Theobald were complying with a royal summons in respect of a more momentous issue.

IX

'I've summoned you here ahead of my meeting with the archbishop for two reasons,' King Henry announced to the three men down one side of the table at which he sat at the head. 'The first is to be advised of the full extent of the earl's proposals for a new justice system, and the second is to decide precisely how we intend to ensure that the Church cannot resile from them and continue to decide matters in its own courts.'

De Beaumont cast a nervous sideways glance at de Lucy, who looked as uncomfortable as he felt. Only William had an air of confidence as he handed copies of his proposed scheme across the table and began.

'The proposal is that the king's justice be administered under a central system of laws that are the same wherever one travels throughout the realm. For example, the taking of a life shall be called "murder", and shall be extensively defined in accordance with a set of principles laid down in an ordinance agreed by the *curia regis*, as the new royal court shall be called. It will be headed by His Majesty, and wherever it sits the effect shall be the same. Whether the court is in Oxford, Westminster, York, Chester or Lincoln, the consequence of taking the life of another shall be death by hanging. It shall be for the *curia* to decide guilt after hearing from the witnesses called in the case.'

'Do we have a complete set of ordinances, laying down the principles of each crime?' de Lucy enquired.

William nodded. 'We shall have, once I have drafted proposals for the *curia* to consider. I should perhaps have added a moment ago that the *curia* upon which these responsibilities will be laid shall be the same council of state that currently meets to advise His Majesty in matters pertaining to the welfare of the nation.'

'So your proposal is that every crime, wheresoever committed, is to be judged by this new court?' de Beaumont enquired sceptically. 'If so, then it will be travelling the nation like tumblers following country fairs, and will have no time for other business.'

'That is where my proposal becomes more challenging,' William went on. 'Clearly the *curia* can only deal with a fraction of all cases, and my further idea is that its functions be devolved upon a body of men appointed by His Majesty who will tour the nation as representatives of the "King in Curia". Given their function, I propose that they be named justices, and that they visit each major town within the realm several times a year in order to deal with the most serious of crimes reserved for them by the local sheriff. The lesser crimes may be left with the sheriffs and the manor courts, as at present, but the most serious — and I have in mind murder, rape, robbery with arms and fire-raising, for example — will be held back for the attention of these newly appointed royal justices. By this means, the king is seen to be dispensing justice evenly but firmly throughout the land.'

'You would be placing a great deal of trust in those appointed to the task,' de Lucy observed thoughtfully. 'They would need to be men of the utmost integrity, completely beyond all suspicion of partiality or malice. Do we have such men available?'

Henry shot him a venomous look as he enquired frostily, 'Is it your opinion that my council is full of dishonest knaves who seek only to feather their own nests?'

'Far from it, sire,' de Lucy hastened to assure him. 'For myself, I have only ever acted in the best interests of England and your honoured self.'

'Then perhaps you would be a suitable person to be sent around the nation dispensing the royal justice?' Henry suggested gleefully, and de Lucy's face paled. He stared down at the table and drew in his shoulders, as if trying to make himself invisible.

William noted his discomfort and came partly to his rescue. 'It might be possible to appoint, as visiting justices, those who already reside in the locality. For example, we could divide the entire nation into what might be termed "justice regions", with a central court to which the justice travels from his nearby estate. Take East Anglia as a test for my notion. If the court were to be held in Norwich, it could hear cases from the whole of East Anglia, with those accused of crime being brought to a prison constructed for that purpose. The appointed justice could then be a prominent and trustworthy baron whose estates are in Norfolk, Suffolk, Cambridgeshire, or even Lincolnshire.'

'I like this idea,' Henry said before there could be any further objection, 'but I would enquire whether it is your proposal that these justices hear cases other than those of serious crime. What of disputes over property, taxation, inheritances and suchlike?'

'That would be a matter for you, sire,' William replied. 'I am merely proposing the administrative structure upon which future justice could be dispensed.'

'You have thus far remained largely silent, Robert,' Henry said to de Beaumont. 'As one of my justiciars you would be championing the new arrangement, should we agree upon it.

Either voice all your doubts now, or forever remain silent about them.'

De Beaumont shrugged. 'I can, at this stage, find no argument against the concept, and William is to be congratulated for the clarity of his thinking. But like Richard, I remain hesitant about placing so much power in the hands of one man, or a series of such men.'

'They enjoy that power already,' William reminded him. 'The reason why His Majesty has set me the task of devising an alternative is that under the present system the barons have the power of life and death in their own courts, interpreting the law as they see fit, and in so doing they provoke much resentment among the people. They also appear to possess an authority that detracts from the crown's. Under my system, all justice flows from the king, and even those barons chosen as justices are answerable to His Majesty for the manner in which they conduct themselves.'

'On the subject of accountability,' Henry interposed, 'what about the clergy? At present, being in holy orders would seem to be the means by which to commit the most heinous of crimes and be punished merely with a penance of laughable ease, such as reading prayers out loud for hours on end.'

'It was my intention that *all* men be answerable to these new laws, sire,' William replied with alarm. 'How can it be seen to be a just system if some men are excused from the consequences of their crimes, merely because they wear a cassock rather than a tunic?'

De Beaumont and de Lucy nodded vigorously in agreement, and Henry appeared pleased with the response.

'I happen to share that opinion,' he said, 'which is why I have summoned Archbishop Theobald to an audience with us. He is without, attended by some monk who assists him to remain upright, and I propose that you all join me in impressing upon him that the clergy must be encompassed within our new justice system.'

A page was sent out into the hall, and shortly thereafter the ageing and grey-faced Archbishop of Canterbury limped in. One age-spotted hand gripped the cane that assisted his steps, while his other hand was clutching the arm of a tall, sturdy-looking monk who smiled affectionately at William as he led Theobald to his seat and lowered him into the chair.

'I must apologise for the fact that God has, in His infinite wisdom, seen fit to give me bodily infirmities that hinder my movements,' Theobald explained. 'Fortunately he has also provided me with Brother Benedict, who attends to my needs in that regard. I ask that he be allowed to remain for that purpose only, and I can vouch for his integrity and silence regarding any matter that we may discuss. I might also add that he is related in close degree to one who is already present.'

All eyes shifted from one to the other until William gave a chuckle. 'Brother Benedict is, in his earthly manifestation, my brother Alain,' he revealed. 'We are in fact twins.'

Henry raised a quizzical eyebrow. 'You hardly resemble each other, but no matter. We may proceed as the archbishop suggests, and I ask that William explains to his Grace what he proposes for the future of English justice.'

William repeated the proposals he had outlined earlier, to which the archbishop listened with apparent equanimity. Then he raised rheumy eyes down the table towards Henry and asked, 'Why am I being consulted in this matter, sire? It seems eminently just that all men be subject to the same laws, and that they be administered equally throughout the nation.'

It fell silent, and it was left to Henry to explain. 'The proposal is that even those who have been ordained, and indeed even those who have merely taken holy orders, will be as accountable as the lowest field labourer or the mightiest lord.'

'Are they not already?' Theobald queried, and Henry looked to William to explain further.

'As I understand it, your Grace, the clergy are tried in their own courts. This cannot continue if we are to see justice dispensed to all, without fear, favour or special treatment.'

'They are *God's* courts,' Theobald objected.

'Administered by senior clergy, who impose penalties for wrongdoing that are inconsistent with those suffered by other men,' William persisted.

'They are in some cases considered *most* severe by those subject to them,' Theobald countered, adding, 'I doubt that Your Majesty would regard three weeks on a diet of bread and water as a light punishment.'

Henry's face reddened, and William braced himself for one of the king's notorious blasts of rage. But he was clearly controlling himself with a massive effort as he replied, 'If a weaver, blacksmith or fuller takes the life of another, he hangs. Likewise even a powerful baron of the realm. If a monk does the same thing, he is set to mumbling a number of *pater nosters,* and all is forgiven. This cannot be allowed to continue.'

'It is what God ordains.'

'It is not what *I* ordain!' Henry thundered.

The archbishop appeared unmoved. 'Do you see yourself as more powerful than God, my son?'

'If I might cite one example of what concerns His Majesty,' William intervened quickly, if only to preserve the Archbishop of Canterbury from being taken out and disembowelled, 'there was the matter of the poisoning of the Archbishop of York.'

'That was during the reign of the previous king,' Theobald objected, but William was not about to be silenced.

'Indeed it was, and it was a prime example of the evil that can overtake the nation when a king loses control of the justice process. The person accused of the crime was Osbert of Bayeux, his own archdeacon, and the poison was allegedly administered through the Communion chalice, over which Osbert had sole control. You were the one who succeeded in having the matter transferred to an ecclesiastical court, before which Osbert was as unable to prove his innocence as others were to prove his guilt. The matter was therefore sent upwards to a papal court, where, for all we know, the matter still lingers, unheard.'

'Several points, if I may,' Theobald responded with a confident smile. 'The first is that both the victim and the accused person were ordained according to the rites of the Church of Rome, which made it entirely an ecclesiastical matter. Secondly, the progress of the judgment through the court of his Holiness the Pope was delayed by the deaths of both King Stephen and Pope Adrian. Finally, the accuser claimed trial by ordeal, which is forbidden to clergy under canon law.'

'Precisely!' Henry yelled. 'You argue against your own case, my lord Archbishop! The very excuses you call in aid only serve to underline the evil of allowing a man to escape the consequences of taking a life simply because he wears a cassock!'

'It is a matter for the Pope,' Theobald insisted.

'And you are the Pope's man here in England,' Henry reminded him, 'so lose no time in advising him that in this country, we play the justice game according to *my* rules, and not his.'

'I will undertake to seek his guidance,' Theobald replied meekly. 'I can do no more than that.'

'At least ensure that you do no *less*!' Henry demanded. 'You are now excused.'

William also excused himself briefly and scuttled out after the archbishop and Alain for long enough to invite the latter to meet his newborn nephew over supper. When he returned to the meeting chamber, the other two were in the process of collecting their papers and taking their leave.

Henry beckoned for William to remain, and when they were alone he asked, 'Have you discussed your proposals with the chancellor?'

'Not yet, sire, since I clearly required your approval before taking any further steps.'

'Return here after dinner, and we shall see what Becket has to say,' Henry requested, and William also took his leave.

As he caught up with de Beaumont and de Lucy in the hallway, de Beaumont looked pale as he commented, 'Theobald is lucky not to be swinging from a palace flagpole. It is to be hoped that the Pope does not delay considering our proposals.'

'Assuming that Theobald even puts them to him,' de Lucy reminded them darkly. 'These are not good times to be disobeying Henry.' He lowered his voice and looked furtively from side to side. 'It is rumoured that Henry has taken a mistress, and that the queen has withdrawn from his company.'

The afternoon meeting with Chancellor Becket was far more amiable, mainly because Thomas seemed willing to agree to everything that was put to him. William explained how the new court system would work, and Henry added that they were unsure whether or not to give the new justices jurisdiction over civil matters. Becket enthusiastically urged that they do so.

'If we have the weight of the royal will behind every judgment,' he explained, 'and if the law is applied consistently in all parts of the kingdom, then my duties will become easier overnight. We can introduce standard forms of land charter, dispositions both *inter vivos* and *post mortem*, advowsons, bonds and suchlike, and know not only what they will contain, but also that they may be enforced. The increase in sums flowing to the Exchequer, and hence onward to the Treasury, will be well worth the administrative upheaval in implementing such changes.'

'Will you work with William to devise the administrative system, and draft these standard charter forms to which you refer?' Henry enquired.

Becket nodded. 'It would be both an honour and a pleasure, sire.'

Henry beamed. 'It is also a pleasure for me to know that your thoughts accord so readily with mine. Now, tell me, since you are in holy orders, what think you of the continuing practice of the clergy being tried in ecclesiastical courts?'

Thomas frowned as he formulated a suitably diplomatic response. 'I know that you met with the archbishop earlier today, and there is tittle-tattle in the halls that the meeting was not all sweetness and light. I hear that Archbishop Theobald is opposed to any change in procedure, and of course I must, in my clerical capacity, submit meekly and humbly to whatever he decrees, in the same way that I bow to your every wish in temporal matters.'

'You have the forked tongue of a diplomat,' Henry smiled, although there was tension at the corners of his mouth. 'You would therefore argue that the clerical courts should continue?'

'I say only that if the Primate of All England says that they must, and his Holiness the Pope gives his support, then short of putting aside my holy vestments I would be obliged to ignore any reservations I might personally entertain.'

Henry smiled conspiratorially. 'And if you *were* his Holiness, or perhaps the archbishop?'

'Then I would clearly be free to follow my own conscience in the matter, sire.'

The meeting ended. As the door closed behind Becket, Henry looked down the table at William.

'What did we just agree?' he asked.

William shrugged. 'Simply that the chancellor does as he is told, sire. We have no idea, at this stage, what he would do were he the one making the decisions.'

'As I thought,' Henry muttered.

'He's a beautiful child,' Alain murmured as he held baby Hugh in his arms and pronounced a simple blessing in Latin. He then planted a kiss on his forehead. Adele stood behind him, itching to take her infant back, and William turned from the table at which he'd been pouring them all a mug of wine.

'I'm sorry we couldn't welcome you to our own estate,' he said, 'but it's four days' hard ride from here, and with a child in our arms it would take much longer. You'll just have to put up with our suite of chambers here at Oxford.'

Alain gave an ironic chuckle. 'If you could see my simple cell inside the monastery at Canterbury, you wouldn't be apologising like that. In any case, just being with family is reward in itself, regardless of where it takes place. It's all very well having God as your Heavenly father, but it doesn't make up for the flesh and blood of loved ones, and of course I'll never have children of my own.'

'If you ever become a parish priest you could,' William said suggestively, 'from what I've heard of their scant regard for the vow of chastity.'

'Well, I'm not,' Alain reminded him in a slightly admonishing tone, 'and in Canterbury we live under the very nose of the head of the English Church, so there's even less opportunity for that sort of thing. But on occasions like this evening, I miss having family close at hand. You have a wife and child, and all I had was an uncle, who we shared, of course. Tell me more about him, at least. I can only recall a fierce-looking man who visited us in the priory at Walsingham, and again at Ely, although when I encountered him briefly in Winchester he seemed less fierce.'

'That's the effect of our respective ages, of course,' William confirmed as there was a knock on the chamber door and Adele beckoned in the servers with the loaded supper trays. 'We grew into adults as he mellowed with advancing years. Our mother was his sister, and her name was Elinor. Through them both we have a very interesting line of descent that our uncle once told me all about, insofar as he could remember what our grandfather had told him.'

'We have the entire evening until I have to rejoin the archbishop for a late Mass and an early retirement,' Alain smiled, 'so please tell. I can at least dream of a life beyond the cloister.'

'Well, our grandfather was called Sir Thomas Walsingham, who was of the estate there. He served the former King Henry as Captain of the Palace Guard, an office not unlike the one that got our uncle killed recently. I assume that you received my letter regarding that, since I knew only that you were somewhere in holy orders in Canterbury.'

'Yes, I did, for which I have not had an opportunity to thank you. But Walsingham was where we were first raised, in the local priory. If Sir Thomas was the lord of the manor there, why do I have no memory of servants, a manor house and all the other trappings of nobility?'

'He was hardly of the nobility, and in fact the manor of Walsingham was never his. It was willed by our great-grandfather Wilfrid, who was Thomas's father, to the prior of the church in which we were raised, since he always maintained that it belonged by rights to the prior's mother. Have I succeeded in completely confusing you yet?'

'Not yet, but continue with the line of ascent — I understood you to say that the estate had once belonged to our family.'

'That's correct, and this is where the family history acquires a more romantic flavour. Sir Wilfrid Walsingham, our great-grandfather, acquired the estate when he was knighted by William of Normandy, and he lived to serve both of his sons during their reigns — the second William, and after him the first Henry.'

'He fought in William's army?'

'Eventually. But prior to that he stood against his invasion force when it attacked near the village in which he was born and raised, as the son of the local miller. The village was called "Sandlake", and he was born simple "Will Riveracre". From there he rose by virtue of a strong sword arm to become a knight under the Norman kings. We come from a long line of warriors, Alain, of which Uncle Richard seems destined to have been the last, since you are in holy orders, and I serve the king as a lawyer rather than as a knight.'

'Thank God that it transpired in that fashion,' Alain muttered as he made the sign of the cross, 'since I could never imagine myself sinking a weapon into the flesh of a fellow human being. And while I hardly knew my uncle well enough to mourn his passing during a brutal siege in a far-off place, I would have cause to shed rivers of tears were I to lose a twin brother whose reacquaintance I have only just made. Let us pray for an enduring peace.'

'Amen to that,' William murmured in response. 'But remember that it is only through the offices of ambassadors, diplomats and lawyers such as myself that peace is maintained. If it were left to kings to wage war like unruly children arguing over a toy, then the world as we know it would be piled high with corpses.'

X

Henry was not concerned to be summoned to the queen's apartments so late in the evening. He was merely annoyed that she thought she could command his presence in such a manner, but also curious as to what might be the reason for it. She had already angrily confronted him with the rumours regarding his trysts with Rosamund Clifford in the gardens of Woodstock, and he had reminded her that even were they true, kings traditionally had mistresses. Her venomous retort had been that kings who kept mistresses only did so because there was nothing available to them in the marital bedchamber, and if that was the way he preferred it, then so be it. But if it wasn't that, then it was probably the same issue that had been troubling him ever since the latest word had come from France, for which he had no ready answer.

Adele slipped diplomatically through the adjoining door into the bedchamber as Henry appeared in the outer chamber and demanded to know why he had been summoned. 'It is for kings to summon queens, and not the other way about. Pray consider that the next time that you wish to converse with me.'

'I do not care for your protocol, Henry,' Eleanor snarled. 'Tell me what you intend to do regarding the latest insult from Louis.'

It was the matter he had feared, and he had not yet formulated an appropriate response. There was, however, no harm in testing the depth of Eleanor's information.

'What might that be, apart from his insistence on remaining alive?'

'You know full well what, so do not pretend. He has married off my daughters without even consulting me. That is an insult to me, and therefore an insult to England and you.'

Henry could hardly deny that. Louis had lost his second wife Constance — not by annulment this time, but by her untimely death in childbirth. The child, a daughter named Alys, had survived, but, desperate for a son, Louis had remarried only five weeks later, this time to Adela of Champagne. At twenty, she was barely half Louis' age. His primary motivation was rumoured to be the need to sire a male heir, but this did not prevent him taking territorial advantage of the two daughters of marriageable age who had been born during his first marriage to Eleanor.

They were named Marie and Alix, and Louis had betrothed each of them to powerful potential allies of France who were also brothers of his new bride. Marie was set to become Countess of Champagne by marriage to Henry, its count, while Alix would become Countess of Blois when she married Theobald V. Strategically it was a serious challenge to England, since Champagne guarded the Île-de-France on its eastern borders, while Blois blocked the road into the Vexin from Henry's lands in Anjou and Maine. Not only was Louis adding to his territorial alliances, but he was also building a defensive ring around Paris and significantly increasing the size of what he insisted on calling 'France'.

'Well?' Eleanor demanded as she drummed her left foot testily on the carpet. 'What do you propose by way of reprisal?'

'What did you have in mind?' Henry replied sarcastically, only to be taken aback by the wisdom of her reply.

'You seize the Vexin — now! Not only will this action block any movement of armed forces out of Blois to assist Louis, but it will also leave a clear route into the Île-de-France from Normandy.'

Henry's mouth opened in admiration, but he was not about to make any concession regarding who controlled his empire. 'For someone whose primary duty is the bearing and nurturing of the next generation of Angevins, you demonstrate an unnerving, and somewhat unladylike, grasp of military tactics.'

'Someone has to, Henry, while you play at being king.'

'May I take it that my summons here was not the result of any carnal desire on your part?'

'You may. Come back when you have demonstrated your suitability for manly pursuits. Beginning with the Vexin.'

'You forget that it will become mine anyway when Henry marries Margaret.'

'If he still wishes to do so, when they are of an age,' she replied dismissively. 'Since you insisted on bringing her back to England with us, she has made a pretty playmate for your favourite son in their nursery, but who would want to marry their infant companion?'

'And what makes you imagine that he has any choice in the matter? If it comes to that, why do we not marry them off immediately?'

Eleanor looked thunderstruck. 'Henry is only five years old, and as for little Margaret, she is barely walking! It was bad enough that you married off our dear little Matilda to that oaf of Germany when she was only ten, but surely Margaret cannot be lawfully married while she is still in napkins?'

'As to that, I shall take the advice of my able legal guide, William of Repton. If it be legally possible, then I shall make it happen.'

Eleanor glared back at him in disgust. 'Thank God that our daughters Eleanor and Joan do not seem to have attracted suitors, else you would also use them for your own ends. As it is, you must perforce rely on your sons — and God knows you have enough of those, thanks to me.'

'We could perhaps make room for one more,' Henry leered. 'I shall return tomorrow at this time. Ensure that you are then resolved to perform your queenly duties.'

'You disgust me!' Eleanor all but spat as Henry turned and stalked out of the chamber with a throaty chuckle of anticipation.

Adele had taken the elementary precaution of listening to the bad-tempered royal exchanges from behind the partially open door between the chambers, and William had therefore been well prepared for the summons two days later. Henry had since persuaded Queen Eleanor that the marriage of Young Henry and Margaret of France would at least provide some vestige of justification for the immediate seizure, on his order, of those fortresses in the Vexin that constituted her dowry.

The only resistance would be likely to come from Simon de Montfort, but given the recent intermarriages involving his house and the English houses of Chester and Leicester, this would be likely to remain merely token in nature. No doubt a loud protest would be sent to Louis of France, who in turn would demand an explanation. Henry was hopeful that he could insist that the lawful marriage of his son to Louis' daughter invoked the terms of their peace agreement, which made provision for England to occupy the Vexin. But before that could happen, a lawful marriage had to be organised.

'Can the marriage between my son Henry and Margaret of France be celebrated immediately, despite their young age?' Henry asked William.

William screwed up his face in pretended thought. In reality he already had most of the answers, thanks to a morning's research in the offices of both the justiciar and the chancellor. 'It can,' he replied guardedly, 'provided that the Pope grants a dispensation.'

'And how would you propose that we set about obtaining one?' Henry enquired eagerly.

'One would normally proceed through the good offices of the Archbishop of Canterbury. However, before they left here to return to Canterbury, my brother was obliged to hire a litter, since his Grace was no longer capable of riding a horse. I have since received word from Alain that Archbishop Theobald has taken to his bed, and is no longer capable of conducting the Masses in his own cathedral.'

'So if the old fool is dying, how may we approach Rome for the dispensation that I need?'

'I put that question to Tom Becket, who as you may know once served in the same monastery as my brother. Whilst in the employ of the archbishop, he made several trips to Rome and made the acquaintance of various bishops who regularly act as what they call papal legates. These are representatives of the Pope, to whom tasks are delegated. Tom believes that the Pope is currently so engaged in an attempt to recruit volunteers for another Crusade that he might be persuaded to leave the matter of your dispensation to a legate. It will then simply be a matter of ensuring that the legate in question is one with whom Tom enjoys a warm friendship.'

'Instruct him to depart for Rome without delay.'

'He has already left, sire. I hope you will forgive me, but I thought his offer was so generous, and was so fearful that he might change his mind, that I instructed him to travel to Dover without delay, and there take ship for Calais, and hence to Rome.'

Henry nodded. 'You have done well, William. So well, in fact, that I will overlook your presumption in passing on an order that I had not even given. But see that it does not happen again.'

Five weeks later Tom Becket reappeared in Oxford, proudly bearing the necessary dispensation. Two months after that, in November 1160, the two infants Henry and Margaret became husband and wife in a brief but sumptuous ceremony in Neubourg, a comfortable day's ride from Evreux and almost within sight of the Vexin that was the young bride's dowry. Having been well behaved during the ceremony, the children were given permission to play, under supervision, on the grassy slope that ran gently down from the castle keep.

Two years passed, during which Henry had replaced the garrisons inside his newly acquired Vexin fortresses with English men at arms. Having given the matter much thought, he called Tom Becket to the Audience Chamber inside Woodstock Palace in order to give him the thanks that had somehow been overlooked in the excitement of the wedding preparations and the events that had followed it.

'It has been some time now since your triumphant return from Rome, Thomas,' Henry began. He handed him a mug of wine and indicated that he should take a seat alongside him by the roaring fire. 'I had always intended to thank you in some suitable way, and now the perfect opportunity has presented itself.'

'Sire?'

'You will of course have learned of the death of Archbishop Theobald?'

'Indeed. A worthy man who led a blameless life, and who always put the Church before any other consideration.'

'I wish you to succeed him.'

There was an ominous silence, during which Becket's eyes were fixed firmly on the carpet. Henry was just convincing himself that the elevation had left Becket speechless with joy when the man looked up and shook his head sadly.

'You do me great honour, sire, and I must apologise most profusely for what will seem to you like ingratitude, but I am neither qualified for, nor worthy of, a position of such importance to the nation.'

'Nonsense, Thomas!' Henry blustered. 'You have served me faithfully and well. I could not wish to have a more worthy servant of the nation as the leader of its Church — God's representative here in our treasured land.'

A further pause made Henry hopeful that his words had caused Becket to rethink his original position, but his hopes were dashed by a more detailed explanation from the reluctant prelate.

'It has always been my motivation in life to work for the best interests of those I serve without reservation and without regard to the cost to myself. I hope that in the discharge of my duties as chancellor I have demonstrated that virtue.'

'Indeed you have, Thomas, indeed you have. This is why I wish you to work equally in my interests while leading the Church here in England.'

'But then I would also be serving God. I am not entirely sure that in so doing I could best serve your interests, if that is why I am being offered such an exalted promotion from that of humble monk to Primate of All England.'

'But you already serve God, do you not? You are already in holy orders.'

'That is not the same thing, sire. As a mere monk I simply follow a daily life of prayer, self-denial and study of the Scriptures. I am not even ordained.'

'So we will get you ordained — wherein lies the problem?'

'Because then I will be bringing God to the people in their daily lives — baptising infants, joining couples in marriage, hearing confessions and so on. God will be my new master, and, knowing my own temperament, I will be driven to serve His best interests. I cannot at this time convince myself that they are also *your* best interests.'

'But if you retain the chancellorship, you will also be sworn to work in my best interests, so can you not carry each of us on your ample shoulders?'

Becket looked horrified. 'You wish me to serve God and Mammon *both* at the same time?'

Henry smiled. 'I recall, during a previous conversation, that you quoted a line from Scripture. It was, as I remember it, "Give what is Caesar's to Caesar". You would not cease to do that, in your role as chancellor, simply because you were also Archbishop of Canterbury?'

Thomas shook his head with a frown. 'That was an incomplete rendering of a well-known line from the Scriptures. It also says, "Give what is God's to God".'

'So, if you serve two masters loyally, and each receives what is due to them, where is the difficulty?'

'There is none, in the normal way of things,' Becket confirmed. 'But what if the two should be in competition?'

'That could not happen, surely?' Henry argued. 'To God go devotion, prayer and tithes. To me comes everything else.'

'That is, with respect, a somewhat simplistic assessment of the dilemmas likely to confront anyone seeking to give leadership to both the Chancery and the Church,' Thomas replied reflectively. 'I cannot of course disobey my king, but I earnestly beseech you not to place me in a situation in which my conscience might be my downfall.'

'You are correct in that, at least,' Henry advised him as the smile froze on his face. 'You cannot disobey your king, and your king will shortly announce your appointment as Archbishop of Canterbury. I have every faith in your ability to serve God.'

'So do I,' Becket replied gloomily as he rose, bowed and backed out towards the chamber door. 'And that is what I fear.'

It was the fastest promotion in the history of the English Church. On 2nd June 1162, in front of the high altar in Canterbury Cathedral, Thomas Becket, a forty-two-year-old monk and Chancellor of England who had begun his life in London's Cheapside, was ordained as a priest. On the following day, before the same altar, he was consecrated as Archbishop of Canterbury by the elderly Bishop of Winchester, Henry of Blois, brother of the former King Stephen. But as the popular former archdeacon walked solemnly in procession out of the cathedral to the cheers of townsfolk and monastery clergy, he could hear another sound above the clamour. It was the cold cawing of black crows perched high in the trees, and in the depths of his heart he knew it to be an omen.

XI

'She's almost as beautiful as her mother,' Alain cooed as he looked down at William's second child, Joan, now almost three years old. They were seated in the summer sunshine under the eaves of Repton Manor, where William and Adele were making the most of the two months' leave of Court granted to them ahead of what each of them must then take on. For Adele it would be a journey across the Channel, accompanying her mistress Queen Eleanor to Poitou, where she hoped to escape from Henry's almost sadistic attempts to get her pregnant for the ninth time during their marriage. Their latest son, John, had been born on Christmas Eve 1166, and Eleanor considered that she had done her duty for England. William, to be left behind in England, had been charged with the laborious and politically fraught task of drafting a new set of constitutions to govern the relationship between the newly instigated 'assize' system of criminal justice and the courts maintained by the Church.

'How old is Hugh now?' Alain enquired as Adele tactfully removed Joan from his arms. He looked across the lawn, where the sturdy boy was chasing a ball he had failed to catch when it had been thrown to him by Thomas Derby, the steward's teenage son.

'He'll be seven on his next birthday,' William replied as he followed Alain's gaze. 'Were either of us that energetic at his age?'

Alain chuckled. 'If we had been, Prior Geoffrey would have hauled us back into line and given us a stern lecture on appropriate deportment inside a house of God. I sometimes catch myself using his very words when I admonish our novices for being too boisterous in the cloisters.'

'You don't regret taking holy orders as a way of life?' William asked, uncomfortably aware of his own sensual nature, and wondering how a man who was his twin managed to suppress carnal yearnings.

'I've never known any other,' Alain reminded him, 'since you were always the outgoing one, curious about life outside the priory, and then the abbey school. I might ask you if you regret going out into the wicked world.'

'Never,' William replied as he reached up and grasped Adele's hand where she stood beside his chair, holding Joan in her arms. 'I am the first to admit that marriage was not high on my agenda when the suggestion was put to me, but I soon learned that there is no greater comfort to a man than a loving wife.'

'He's talking nonsense, as usual,' Adele grinned. 'He married me because I came with an estate.'

'Our uncle did the same, apparently,' William advised Alain. 'Did you know that?'

'I assume that it was a different estate, with a different wife?' Alain joked.

William laughed. 'Of course — the estate was Chalfont, down near London, and the widow who he married was called Agnes. Sadly, she passed with her latest ague some months ago now, but prior to that they said that she was declining fast after Uncle Richard's death. But back to your current dry life under monastic rules — how are things under your new archbishop?'

'This is probably the appropriate time to tell you, since you raise the matter,' Alain began proudly, 'that your twin brother is now an Archdeacon of Canterbury.'

'Excellent!' William grinned with genuine pleasure. 'That, if I remember correctly, is a highly prestigious office, but one that requires its holder to conduct endless Masses at different hours of the day while his archbishop remains in his bed.'

'Not *this* archbishop,' said Alain. 'Thomas Becket is an inspiration to us all, and quite unlike his predecessor, even allowing for his age and bodily infirmities. Our new prelate conducts all the Masses, spends countless hours in devotions of his own in his private chapel, and even wears a hair shirt that is rumoured to be crawling with lice, just to mortify the flesh. It is impossible to believe that he was not even ordained until the day before his consecration, such is his knowledge and understanding of cathedral life, his devotion to his flock and his concern for the local town community. It's as if he craves sainthood *before* he dies.'

'He may well acquire martyrdom if he defies King Henry over his latest ambitions regarding the Church courts,' William replied gloomily. 'He has already angered Henry by resigning his chancellorship without seeking leave, or even paying Henry the courtesy of advising him in advance of his intentions. Now I hear that he has begun instructing the bishops to defy any attempt to have clergymen who commit crimes hauled before the king's courts. How can he continue to justify an arrangement under which someone who commits a crime for which others would hang can get away with a flogging at worst, or a period of imprisonment with bread and water?'

'The Church has long claimed the right to try its own,' Alain argued, 'since the days when men were put to death for the most trivial of alleged offences, such as insulting the royal person by farting in their presence.'

'That is surely an exaggeration!' William laughed.

Alain shook his head. 'It has been known, William. As you know, we in the service of God abhor even the spilling of blood, let alone the taking of life — whatever the offence — and our court system exists to ensure that our own brethren are sheltered from such brutality.'

'But therein lies the source of conflict with the temporal authorities,' William reminded him. 'Henry does not challenge the right of a man in holy orders to be adjudged guilty or not by one of your courts, but his argument is that if that man be found guilty, he should be defrocked, or whatever the expression is — stripped of his holy status, anyway — and handed over for punishment under royal justice.'

Alain sighed as he repeated the well-worn counterargument. 'If we were to do that, then ours would be the decision that led to a man being put to death, maimed, branded or whatever. You can understand our reluctance.'

'I can understand it, certainly, but please warn your archbishop that he is heading for certain loss of office, *and* a possible final visit to the Tower of which Henry is growing so fond, if he continues to defy him in the matter.'

'And *you* are heading for a regimen of bread and water if you don't stop haranguing your brother about matters over which he has no control,' Adele advised William. 'Now, lead us in to dinner.' After ordering Hugh off the lawn, she walked into the house with Joan still in her arms.

William and Adele travelled back down to the Court at Oxford after leaving young Hugh in the care of the estate steward. Then, after a gloomy few days of contemplating what lay ahead, and a predictably tearful farewell, Adele, with little Joan in her arms, rejoined the queen's entourage as it set off for Portsmouth on its long journey to Poitou. William tried to fill his time with last-minute preparations for the council meeting that Henry had summoned at Clarendon, his favoured hunting lodge in Wiltshire.

It was Henry's belief that the final proposal drafted by William was a generous compromise that allowed the Church to retain its primary authority over those in holy orders who committed criminal acts. They might, he conceded, assess guilt or otherwise as the primary court of judgment, but if found guilty the offender must be handed over to the newly appointed king's justices for sentence. While everyone else around the council table was prepared to go along with this and move on to other matters, there were groans of frustration when Becket refused to agree.

'He's in a minority of one,' Justiciar de Beaumont pointed out. 'Not even the Bishop of Winchester agrees with him, so let's just pass these constitutions that the Earl of Repton has drafted most excellently and get on with the other business. It will soon be dinner time, and my stomach is rumbling already.'

'There are more important issues at stake here than the state of your gut,' Becket sniffed disapprovingly. 'I have two fundamental objections to what is being proposed. The first is that the ultimate authority over those who have taken holy orders is not His Majesty, but his Holiness the Pope.'

'Treason!' de Beaumont hissed, to a background of supporting murmurs.

Becket pierced him with a stony glare. 'May I continue?'

'You may continue to a traitor's death on the gallows,' de Beaumont spat, but it seemed that nothing would shift the calm and determined expression on the archbishop's face as he continued.

'My other objection is more legal in nature. If a man be held guilty in a Church court, he must be punished in the manner laid down under the principles of his Order. That may be a flogging, a period of isolation, or even a de-ordination — what some call "de-frocking". But if he is then to be taken out and hanged, mutilated or whatever, then not only is that an act of barbarity against which the Church must set its face, but the unfortunate offender will thereby be punished a second time. I understand that two punishments for the one offence offend even your own laws, which are in other ways inhuman in the extreme.'

'You deny the right of His Majesty to pass laws to protect his own subjects?' de Lucy asked with a crafty smile across the table at de Beaumont, who nodded quietly in response.

Becket considered his answer before delivering it. 'I deny the right of any man to deprive another of his life. The Scriptures tell us that "Thou Shalt not Kill", and those words come from God himself.'

There were several nervous intakes of breath, not least from William, who could readily appreciate the corner into which Becket had been manoeuvred. Everyone looked towards Henry, whose face had gone pale, whether in anger or not it was impossible to tell. But by a supreme effort he controlled his emotions, and merely announced that the meeting was suspended until the following day. He then turned to Becket. 'Thomas, take a turn with me through our beautiful gardens.'

It remained ominously quiet for a lengthy period as the king and the archbishop strolled side by side across the lawns towards the beech coppice.

Henry finally spoke. 'You are a man of high intelligence, Thomas — you must see that my justiciars are intent upon your downfall.'

'They must do as their conscience bids them, Henry, as must I.'

'I raised you from nothing, first to chancellor, then to the foremost clerical position in the land.'

'And, as you may recall,' Becket murmured, 'I almost begged you not to do so. I know my own nature, and it drives me to serve, with every fibre in my body, whomsoever is my master. I now serve God — would you that I serve Him with any less fervour than I once served you?'

Henry sighed, stopped, and took each of Becket's hands in his. 'If you continue to defy the council, they will insist that I have you charged with treason. I will be powerless to refuse, if I wish to retain any vestige of authority as King of England.'

Becket smiled sympathetically as he removed his hands. 'Give what is Caesar's to Caesar and what is God's to God.'

The following day loomed cloudy, with the rumble of thunder in the distant Downs, and everyone took their seats back around the council table with varying emotions. William hung his head and said a silent prayer as Becket continued to defy the others, refusing to give his consent to the constitutions that lay in draft form in front of everyone. Henry announced, in a small, wavering voice that was unlike his normal peremptory boom, that they should move on to other business, including the recent uprisings in Ireland, and the council completed its agenda in time for an early dinner. A notable absentee from the board was Archbishop Becket, who was given leave to return to Canterbury while de Beaumont and de Lucy sought a private audience with the king, from which even William was excluded.

But he found out soon enough what was to follow, when he was instructed to draft a set of allegations against Becket, and summon him to Northampton on a given date in October. There, he would face charges of contempt of royal authority

— a prelude to a possible treason charge — and malfeasance while in office as chancellor. William did so with a doubly heavy heart, since this time — unlike on previous occasions, when she had proved to be a valuable sounding board — he was without the wife he had come to love, and whose opinion he respected because it was always honest. He was also experiencing his first doubts regarding whether or not he wished to be part of the royal system of justice, which seemed to be constructed largely in order to give King Henry whatever he wanted.

With a newly demonstrated flair for the dramatic, Becket appeared before his accusers barefoot, clad only as a simple monk, but carrying his pectoral cross high in the air ahead of him. He easily batted away allegations of misappropriation of Chancery funds that were based on the rich lifestyle he had enjoyed whilst in that office, but he grew more heated when the same accusations were levelled at him regarding certain sums formerly missing from the accounts of the See of Canterbury. He pointed out that his predecessor had grown lax in matters of administration, and that the deficit had already existed when he, Becket, took over the office. Since then, he insisted, the books had been balanced by careful management and a reduction in expenditure, largely on his own table.

The chief accuser, de Beaumont, acting in the king's name, enquired, 'Do you deny that you displayed contempt of His Majesty by refusing to give your agreement to certain new constitutions appertaining to the peace of the realm?'

'I admit to expressing my abhorrence at what was being proposed,' Becket responded defiantly. 'But do you now maintain that expressing a contrary voice to His Majesty's, in the council that is convened to advise him, constitutes contempt?'

'I say,' de Beaumont smiled sadistically, 'that when you openly defy His Majesty's authority to act as the final court of judgment in matters that pertain to the safety of the realm, you show contempt for His Majesty, and disregard for the welfare of his dominions.'

'A matter of interpretation,' Becket shrugged. 'Mere words. Semantics. Lawyer's guile.'

'But however it be interpreted, you do not deny that you claimed that there is an authority higher than His Majesty's?'

'Of course I do not,' Becket replied with confidence, 'else I would not work tirelessly to promote the will of God.'

It fell silent as everyone contemplated the implications. William groaned inwardly as he saw the grimace on de Beaumont's face and heard him begin to pronounce his finding of guilt, despite the fact that there were others designated to share the decision-making.

'I find you guilty, on your own admission…' he began.

Becket raised a hand as if bestowing a blessing on a penitent. 'I cannot hear you, if by implication you will be proclaiming blasphemy.'

'Hear, then, your sentence…' de Beaumont yelled, but was silenced by an angry roar from Becket.

'I will be judged by our Lord the Pope alone, for he alone is competent to judge me, and to him, in your presence, I appeal.' He turned, then stormed from the chamber at twice the speed he had entered it.

In the excited hubbub that followed, de Beaumont beckoned to William, who left the side bench and stood on tiptoe so as to be able to converse with his employer seated on the raised platform.

'Does the fool speak truly when he claims a right of appeal from my judgment?'

'That is a matter I will need to look up,' was all that William could offer.

With a snarl of frustration, de Beaumont left the platform. 'The king shall hear of this!'

The following morning there was no sign of Becket, and nervous servants of Northampton Castle reported that he had reclaimed his horse from the stables the previous evening and ridden hard down the road towards London. William was dispatched to discover whether or not Thomas had sought the intervention of the king at Westminster, but when he made enquiry he was summoned to Henry's Audience Chamber and obliged to recount all that had transpired at Northampton.

'He does his cause no favours,' Henry responded sadly. 'Ride to Canterbury and see if you can prevail upon him to return under my protection, while we sort out the mess he has got himself into.'

At Canterbury William was met by a doleful Alain, who advised him of Thomas's movements. 'The archbishop left for Dover two days since, along with his confessor and a manservant. I can only hope that he is bound for Rome to seek the intercession of his Holiness. In the meantime, it would seem that I am left alone with the burdens of the See on my inadequate shoulders.'

'You know that you relish the opportunity to demonstrate your potential as a bishop,' William teased. 'Did your master reveal all that transpired at Northampton?'

'Not the details, but sufficient to reveal that his life may be forfeit if he remains in England. Would *your* master have the courage to execute such a mighty man of God?'

'Not alone, perhaps,' William replied glumly. 'But there are others surrounding him who would urge him to it, and regrettably they are those by whom I am employed. I take it that it's too late for me to take holy orders?'

'It's never too late for that,' Alain smiled. 'We have men in our monastery old enough to be our father. The question would rather be whether you would be able to commit to a life of poverty, chastity and obedience.'

'Would you accept two out of three?' William grinned back. 'Which only serves to remind me how much I miss Adele. Her devotion to duty took her to Poitiers with the queen, who, so far as I understand it, is also seeking a life of chastity where Henry is concerned.'

'In one sense, it is good that you miss her. Yours must be one of those unions that God has blessed.'

'It's only a pity that He was not so generous regarding how I earn my living,' William grimaced. 'I almost believe what your master had to say about the superiority of God's word, and I despise myself for what I am obliged to do in order to arm his enemies. I was truly humbled when I heard the archbishop's protests regarding the taking of life simply to maintain power.'

'Join me in the refectory for a *real* lesson in humility,' Alain replied. 'Brother Peter's potage is a penance in itself.'

Three years later Henry became incandescent with rage when advised, via urgent letters from the loyal de Montforts in Evreux, that Becket had been given sanctuary by Louis VII, and was safely installed within the cloisters of the Cistercian abbey of Pontigny. Furious protests were relayed by the English envoy in Paris, all of which were ignored. But when Becket fired back by threatening excommunication to all those bishops who implemented the 'Constitutions of Clarendon' that William had drafted, and interdict to the entire nation if Henry persisted in trying clergy in the royal courts, Henry was obliged to reconsider.

He sent word to Pope Alexander III that he was open to a compromise that would allow Becket to return from exile, free of all charges. Papal legates were in the process of wending their way north from Rome when Becket finally went too far. This time, it went beyond mere semantics over the relative authorities of king and God, and struck at the very heart of Henry's dynastic ambitions.

The young Prince Henry was now fifteen years old, and still married to Margaret of France, although given that she was still not yet twelve there were serious doubts regarding whether or not the union had been consummated. Be that as it may, Henry was the oldest son, and his father had bitter memories of the chaos that had followed the uncertainty of his grandfather's bequest of the English crown, first to his nephew Stephen of Blois, and then to his only legitimate heir, Maude. Henry of Anjou was not about to let history repeat itself, and he began preparations for 'the Young Henry' to be crowned during his own lifetime.

The major obstacle in the way of this was tradition, which required a coronation to be conducted by the Archbishop of Canterbury. But it was not unknown for the second Primate of England to do the honours, and Duke William of Normandy himself had been crowned by Aldred, Archbishop of York, on Christmas Day 1066.

On 14 July 1170, in York Minster, its archbishop, flanked by the Bishops of London and Salisbury, made the Young Henry joint monarch with his proud father. Not only was this to prove disastrous for Henry's continued peaceful reign, but it provoked Becket, in exile, into placing England under interdict. This deprived the nation, and all those within it, of the comfort of services such as marriage, baptism and burial. More disturbingly, it absolved all Henry's subjects from any allegiance to him, severing the feudal bonds that held English society together.

This made Henry once again amenable to negotiation and compromise, and he swallowed his pride for long enough to request, under the auspices of Louis of France, a meeting with Becket at Fréteval, on the banks of the Loire and on almost neutral territory in Blois. Becket and Henry approached each other cautiously on horseback, tentatively exchanged the kiss of peace, then begged each other's forgiveness. They agreed that in return for Henry allowing Young Henry to be re-crowned, Becket would withdraw the recent interdict and excommunications and return to his duties in Canterbury.

Henry, much relieved, embarked on a tour of his castles in Normandy, while Becket returned with great pomp, first to Canterbury, then to London, where he distributed alms among the people and was applauded and revered almost like a returning war hero. But it was as if the man was courting martyrdom as he set about rubbing Henry's nose in his recent capitulation.

Almost clairvoyantly, he made an announcement to a horrified congregation during his Christmas Day sermon: 'I am come to die among you.' Then he set about excommunicating all those who had taken advantage of his previous exile, including those bishops who had presided over the coronation of Young Henry, and the joint justiciars de Beaumont and de Lucy. An irate de Beaumont travelled to Normandy in great haste to report Becket's latest provocative actions, and eventually found Henry in a state of advanced inebriation late one evening, surrounded by the usual Anglo-Norman baronial sycophants and hangers-on seeking advancement.

When de Beaumont reported Becket's latest theatrical display Henry flew into one of his wild rages, cursing and blaspheming before turning angrily on de Beaumont.

'What have you done about him?' he demanded.

'Nothing, sire — we were awaiting your instruction,' de Beaumont replied.

Henry gave a roar, hurled his wine goblet at the side tapestries and bellowed, 'This man Becket ate my bread and mocks my favours! He tramples on the whole royal family! What miserable drones and traitors have I nourished and brought up in my household, who let their lord be treated with such shameful contempt by a lowborn clerk!'

Henry was eventually carried out of the chamber, insensibly drunk. But four of his more ambitious knights, still sober, gave orders for their horses to be saddled without delay, and rode north into the night.

They were Reginald FitzUrse, Hugh de Morville, William de Tracy and Richard le Breton, and they were on their way to commit murder.

XII

William had just returned from his Christmas leave of absence while his immediate master de Beaumont was away visiting the king in Normandy, and he could hear the excited chattering from the outer office of the justiciar's chambers before he even reached the door. He pushed his way in, and it fell uneasily silent as the clerks looked nervously, one to another, daring someone to speak.

'What is it?' William demanded wearily. 'Did someone spill more ink? If so, you know the rule — whoever it was can spend however long it takes to clean it up, then stay back later to make up the time.'

'It's not that, sir,' Senior Clerk Howard Clyfton advised him with obvious reluctance.

'Then what? Speak up, man — I'm only just back from my estate up north, and I need to be brought up to date with anything important.'

'It's Archbishop Becket, sir,' another clerk mumbled.

When William raised his eyebrows with impatience, Clyfton added, 'He's dead, sir — murdered. Inside Canterbury, along with one of his archdeacons.'

'One of the Archdeacons of Canterbury has been murdered, you said?'

'Yes, sir — Brother Benedict. But so has the archbishop himself, which is what must be regarded as the most serious news,' Clyfton prompted him, wondering if his master had left his sense of priority behind on his estate.

'Not if you're the brother of the archdeacon in question,' William replied in a voice flat with shock. 'When was this?'

'A few days after Christmas, they reckon,' another clerk chimed in. 'It seems that some knights broke down the door, then hacked the top off his head — in front of all his monks, what's more.'

'Where did this information come from?'

'It's all over the city, sir. A merchant came up from Dover two nights since, carrying the tidings, and it's the talk of the waterfront alehouses.'

'If it's reached the alehouses, then no wonder you piss-pots found out,' William frowned. 'So have the authorities apprehended those responsible?'

'No idea, sir. We only heard ourselves when we called in for breakfast at Molly's Pie Shop. And what with the justiciar being away and all...'

'We have two justiciars,' William reminded them testily. 'Has anyone told de Lucy?'

'He's touring the nation checking on the new criminal assize lists, sir, if you recall,' Clyfton said politely.

'Yes, of course,' William conceded, then made a swift decision that seemed the most appropriate in the circumstances. 'Leave word, should de Lucy return while I'm away, that I've ridden to Canterbury in order to obtain further information, and to ensure that those responsible are brought to justice. Clyfton, you're in charge again in my absence.'

William disappeared out into the hallway, heading for the stables. Tears flowed down his stern face as he urged his galloping horse across London Bridge into Southwark on his way to the Dover Road.

As William clattered into Canterbury after using up three horses on the unbroken day and night journey, its narrow streets looked as if an invading army had laid waste to it. It was now the middle of his second day since leaving Westminster, but the alleys and doorways were all but empty of people, as if the townsfolk were terrified to show their faces. Here and there, small clusters of scared-looking inhabitants were either standing, still immobile from shock, or muttering fearfully among themselves. The door that led through the western entrance into the great nave — the public entrance to the ancient cathedral — was piled high with floral tributes, and interspersed among them were casks of home-grown wine, loaves of bread and sides of meat, as if the dead prelate required sustenance on his undoubted journey into God's welcoming arms.

William turned almost immediately right, through the door that he knew from his last meeting with Alain led to the monks' cloisters, and from there towards the chapter house where the brothers met to discuss material matters to do with the Benedictine monastery that was older even than the cathedral it served. He followed the sound of gentle chanting, and found himself in the tiny chapel dedicated to the founder of the original holy house, St Augustine.

There were thirty or so brothers conducting Mass in muted tones that reflected their sorrow and shock at recent events, and they were being led by an older brother whose face was familiar. He nodded towards William when he saw him standing respectfully at the back door, then turned to give instructions to the younger man by his side, who immediately took over as the older man walked down the side aisle and beckoned William outside with a sympathetic smile.

'I'm Brother James, the sacrist. We have met before, have we not? Your brother on earth was our beloved archdeacon, Brother Benedict?'

'He was,' William replied tersely, not trusting himself to say more as he felt the tears welling up. 'They tell me that he has been promoted to Heavenly glory, or however else you holy men describe it.'

'It was certainly well earned. He was loved by all with whom he came in contact, and he died in an attempt to preserve the life of the most saintly man that God ever put on this earth.'

'How did it happen?' William asked in a voice that was on the point of cracking.

Brother James had a faraway look on his face as he recalled the dreadful event. 'It was four days after Christmas, and the congregation had gathered for the evening Mass. Thomas was kneeling before the altar of St Benedict in the north transept when we heard the sound of men approaching the cathedral through the door that leads from the Great Cloister — the door through which you no doubt entered in order to find us. Your brother led a group of others from our holy house who were about to bar the door, because we could hear these men, who seemed to be drunk, demanding Thomas's presence, and calling him a traitor to the king. Thomas ordered them to leave the door open, because — and I still recall his exact words — "It is not right to make a fortress out of the house of prayer." That was so typical of him.'

He stopped briefly as his voice broke with emotion, and William waited patiently for him to continue.

'Your brother stood in the doorway and asked the men what their business was with the archbishop. They were heavily armed, and clearly intended violence. One of them said that they had come to kill a traitor, and your brother was in the act of arguing with them regarding Thomas's loyalty to the people of England when one of them ran him through with his sword. They then strode over his body and stormed into the transept.'

'He died bravely, it would seem,' William choked.

Brother James nodded. 'He will no doubt be seated on the right hand of God for his bravery. But it was all in vain. Thomas stepped out into the transept, just ahead of the steps that lead to the quire, where some of the brothers had been singing Vespers. The congregation in the nave, who could see what was happening, called upon Thomas to see to his own safety, but to the very end he maintained that he was standing in God's house, and that God would protect him.'

'Had he no fear for his own life?'

'If he did, it didn't show. He was more concerned with refuting the allegations of treachery to the king that the oafs were screaming at him. Then he simply held out his arms, like Christ on the cross, and called out in a loud voice, "For the name of Jesus and the protection of the Church, I am ready to embrace death." In a final act of defiance, he walked back to the altar of St Benedict and knelt before it in prayer.'

'He died there?' William asked.

Brother James nodded, dry-retched at the returning memory, then regained control. 'The first blow took the top off Thomas's head, as one would prepare to eat an egg. Thomas fell forward, and his attackers took it in turns to plunge their swords into his body. It is to be hoped that in His infinite mercy God gave him a swift death. As a final desecration, one of his murderers took the tip of his sword and scooped out the archbishop's brains, and the stain of them still lies before that altar.'

'Where is his body now?'

'It lies in the crypt. Your brother is buried in the brothers' graveyard, to the right of the courtyard on the other side of the cloisters. I may leave you to pay your respects as befits a brother, since his grave has a simple cross at its head, recording his name.'

'Before you return to your devotions, can you give me the names of those responsible for this terrible outrage?' asked William.

Brother James shook his head. 'They were strangers to this town. We knew that they were knights, from their weapons and the richness of their apparel. But they were ragingly drunk, behaving like the worst of animals, and they were only here for long enough to do their wicked deed. They rode off towards Dover, or so we were told by some who were in the street when they left.'

'Thank you anyway,' William said as he felt in his purse for coins. 'I'd like to donate something for your work among the poor.'

'Your family has already given enough,' said Brother James sadly. 'It has lost a brother in God's service.'

'And the other brother will not rest until he has found those responsible and brought them to justice,' William replied through gritted teeth. He thanked Brother James one final time and turned to walk through the cloisters to visit Alain's grave and make him the same promise.

Three days later, back in Westminster, William was advised that de Beaumont had returned from Normandy and wished to speak with him without delay. William was intent on such a meeting anyway, and therefore lost no time in presenting himself at the door to the justiciar's inner chamber.

'You have just returned from Canterbury?' asked de Beaumont.

William nodded grimly. 'I have all the details in my head. There were four of them, and the king must be advised without delay.'

'The king already knows,' de Beaumont advised him. 'I was with him when the news was brought to us at Caen, and I have been sent back in haste, in advance of the news being spread throughout the kingdom.'

'I wish to be the one who hunts them down and brings them to justice,' said William, but de Beaumont shook his head.

'There will be no investigation.'

'But we need to discover who was responsible!' William protested.

De Beaumont looked him sternly in the eye. 'We believe we already know who was responsible.'

'Then why are they not already languishing in chains?'

'For two reasons. The first is that we do not know where they may be skulking. There are conflicting reports, it seems. One version has it that they have fled to Louis' Court in Paris. Another is that they may be found in the Low Countries. Yet another has them in hiding in some castle up north.'

'And the second reason?'

De Beaumont sighed. 'The second reason is that they may have believed that Henry had sanctioned it. That is why I have made an early return, in order to suppress any talk of that nature.'

'Surely, King Henry — for all that the archbishop was a thorn in his side — would not have sent men to slaughter a man of God? *Two* men of God, as it transpires. My brother also died trying to save his master — he was an archdeacon at Canterbury.'

'My sympathies for your loss,' de Beaumont muttered. 'As to your first point, of course Henry would not have commissioned Becket's death, had he been his normal self. But, sad to relate, he was very drunk, and flew into one of his wild rages when he learned of my excommunication, among others. He yelled words that could have been taken as a request for Becket to be done to death.'

'Words which he now regrets?'

'Words which he now *denies*. I was there at the time, and were I to repeat those words — even to you — my head would be forfeit. And so I am sent to spread such denial, and punish with extremity any suggestion that Henry was a party to what happened.'

'And if those responsible were to be caught and tortured, they would no doubt insist that they were carrying out the king's orders?'

'You assess the situation admirably.'

'So they will escape the consequences of their wickedness?'

'Here on earth certainly, if Henry has anything to do with it. Such are my instructions. What tortures may await them in the fires of Hell are, of course, another matter, but you are to do nothing more in this matter, do you clearly understand that? And can you now appreciate *why*? If you set one foot towards unearthing those responsible, you will die a traitor's death, and there is nothing I could do to prevent that.'

'It will be hard for me to obey that instruction,' William glared at de Beaumont, who smiled sympathetically.

'Do you think it is any easier for me? You, at least, can make yourself scarce, whereas I must remain at my post.'

'Why would I need to make myself scarce?' William demanded indignantly. 'I have done nothing wrong.'

'Not yet,' de Beaumont agreed. 'But I fear what you *will* do, if left to stew in your grief for the loss of your brother. He was all the family you had, was he not?'

'Apart from my wife and two children, yes,' William replied gloomily. 'My son resides on my estate, but my wife Adele serves Queen Eleanor in Poitiers, and she has our little daughter with her. Otherwise, yes — I am left to mourn alone.'

'Then perhaps you might wish to visit them,' de Beaumont advised him quietly. 'I can grant you leave to do so. Were you to remain here with such fire of revenge in your belly, you would be sure to forfeit your head. I think too highly of you to allow you to do that. Give Her Majesty my best, and assure her that the nation is well governed while Henry is holding together his many possessions across the Channel.'

'Would you like to go and visit Mother and Joan in Poitou?' William asked twelve-year-old Hugh once the initial hugs, kisses and expressions of mutual joy had been exchanged at their reunion.

Hugh nodded eagerly. 'Will there be dragons and demons there?'

William smiled and looked up at Steward Matthew Derby. 'What sort of nonsense have you been filling the boy's head with, Matthew?'

'Not me, sir — the boys from the estate with whom he sometimes plays, but always under the supervision of my son, of course. The other boys fill his head with stories of knightly deeds, fair maidens in distress and so on. Some of their games can involve pretending to fight, with sticks for swords. I hope you do not disapprove, but boys must be allowed to be boys — it's the only way they grow up to become squires, and then progress to be knights.'

William frowned. 'I'm not sure that I wish him to go down that road, Matthew. Too many of my ancestors perished before their time by such a process — including my own uncle.'

'But I want to be a knight!' Hugh protested.

William ruffled his hair. 'Right at this moment, you need to pack your knightly attire to visit a queen.'

'Does she need rescuing from a wicked baron?' asked Hugh.

William laughed. 'Perhaps — but not quite in the way you mean. Now, go and collect your most precious toys.'

XIII

Two weeks later, William climbed wearily from his horse in the courtyard of the grand Palace of Poitiers, and lifted Hugh down from where he had spent the entire journey wedged in between his father and the forward saddle pommel. He was asleep but came grumpily awake as he was being lifted down, and as usual he complained of feeling hungry. 'But no more monks' potage, please,' he mumbled.

'It has kept you alive since we left home,' William reminded him, 'but perhaps we can find something more substantial in the kitchens of this fine palace. And somewhere inside here we'll also find Mother and Joan, if God is on our side.'

'Are we there at last?' Hugh asked.

William placed him upright on the cobbles. 'We are indeed, no thanks to your constant complaining.'

'I'm still hungry,' Hugh said again, as if this justified his displeasure at what they had endured since leaving Repton.

The kitchen was easily located, given that it was in the courtyard, and the noise coming from it, in the hour before dinner, was both deafening and clamorous. William strolled inside, guiding Hugh by the arm, and asked if there might be some bread and meat available for the boy.

'Who might you be?' a man covered in sweat demanded testily. 'An' by rights, yer shouldn't be in 'ere.'

'We'll only be here briefly,' William explained. 'I'm here in the service of the Justiciar of England, and I seek the Lady Adele, who attends upon Queen Eleanor.'

'Well, yer in the right place,' the man advised him gruffly. 'She'll be down 'ere shortly, ter tell us when the queen's ready fer 'er dinner ter be served, so yer may as well wait 'ere. I'll give the lad some fish while yer wait.'

Ten minutes later, despite all the bustle, shouting, rising steam and confusion, Hugh looked up from where he was hungrily stuffing fish into his mouth and called, 'Mama!' On the other side of the kitchen, where he stood talking to a kitchen hand, William heard Hugh call out and followed the boy's gaze. His eyes met Adele's as she looked through the serving hatch, then disappeared almost instantly. A moment later she raced into the kitchen, bouncing off several kitchen hands with loaded dishes in her anxiety to confirm that she wasn't dreaming. She then gave a joyful squeal and pulled Hugh off his stool and into her arms.

'You'll give the boy a stomach gripe, disturbing his eating like that,' William chided her mockingly as he stepped forward with a tear rolling down his cheek.

'You'll get yours later,' she grinned back at him. 'And if I haven't finally lost my wits through constant yearning, God be praised!'

'What's become of Lady Adele?' Queen Eleanor demanded of the server who was laying the trenchers on the board ahead of dinner. 'She obviously gave word for dinner to be served, but she hasn't returned — has something happened to her?'

'A man in the kitchen, Your Majesty,' the girl replied with downcast eyes.

Eleanor frowned. 'What do you mean, girl? Speak plainly — has she been accosted by a man?'

'Sort of, Your Majesty. There's a young boy there as well, and she's hugging the pair of them and crying her eyes out. I've never seen either of them before, begging your pardon and all.'

'Send her up here immediately — with or without the man and the boy. I'm eager for my dinner.'

The girl scurried back down the serving stairs and along the courtyard to the kitchen, while Eleanor sat with a stony face, surveying the still empty table. After a few moments she heard a woman's hushed voice at the downstairs entrance, followed by the voice of a child asking, 'Will there be roast pork?' There was a scampering sound on the stone steps as a young boy came into view. He halted in the doorway, stared at the table, then called back down, 'There's nothing here but an old woman!'

A red-faced Adele appeared behind him, a look of horror on her face. 'Please forgive him, Your Majesty — he had no idea who you were, and to him everyone aged over twenty is old.'

Eleanor found herself chuckling as she beckoned the boy over. 'What's your name, young man?'

'Hugh, missus.'

'Hugh, *Your Majesty*!' Adele corrected him. 'This is Queen Eleanor, my mistress.'

'Do you have a second name, young Hugh?' Eleanor asked.

'Hugh of Repton, Your Majesty — my father's an earl.'

'And this lady is your mother?'

'Yes, miss — Your Majesty. And Father's downstairs, stabling the horse.'

'Are you hungry, Hugh?'

'Starving, Your Majesty!'

'Well, come and sit here next to me. When they finally get around to serving dinner, you can show me how well you can eat.'

'I fear that his manners at board will not be what Your Majesty is accustomed to,' Adele advised her with a look of alarm.

144

Eleanor laughed. 'You obviously haven't seen my husband eat when he comes in from a hunting expedition. And talking of hungry men, invite your husband to join us as well.'

As the last of the servers bowed out of the chamber some minutes later, Eleanor smiled across at William, who was devoting more time to supervising Hugh at the table than he was to eating.

'Your face is obviously familiar to me, and I know that Adele is your wife, and that this refreshingly normal young man is your son, but remind me — aren't you one of the justiciars in England?'

'I work for them both, yes, Your Majesty.'

'So what is your reason for being here? Has the king sent you to arrest me?'

A look of horror crossed William's face as he hastened to reassure her. 'Nothing of the sort, Your Majesty, I assure you.'

'Then what brings you here, apart from the natural desire to be with your wife and daughter, and of course to remind young Hugh that he has a mother?'

There was an awkward silence before William admitted the truth. 'Have you yet learned of the death of Archbishop Becket?'

Both women looked up from their meals, but it was Eleanor who asked, 'Did his fondness for the austerity of monastic life finally prove his downfall?'

'In a sense, yes, Your Majesty. I regret to have to be the one to advise you that he was done to death in front of his congregation, and before the altar in his side chapel.'

Eleanor looked genuinely horrified. 'Can this be true? Who was responsible for such a vile act?'

'It is certainly true, Your Majesty. I journeyed to Canterbury myself to confirm the report, since my brother was also murdered. He was an archdeacon there, and he died defending his master from the animals who did him to death.'

Adele gave a little squeal and dropped her knife. 'Alain — *dead*?'

'Slaughtered like a pig before Christmas,' William confirmed sadly.

Eleanor looked across at him. 'You have my sincere sympathies for your loss, but why are you here, and not searching for those responsible?'

William hesitated for a moment, then looked down at the board. 'The justiciar declines to investigate the matter.'

'On whose orders? My husband's?' Eleanor asked.

'So I was advised, Your Majesty. It seems that there are ugly rumours that the murder was carried out at his request.'

'Never!' Eleanor protested. 'Henry is all sorts of fool, but he would never order such a serious act. Apart from the fact that in his heart of hearts he both liked and respected Becket, it will send all the wrong messages around Europe if it is trumpeted abroad that he ordered Becket's death. The nation will be placed under interdict, Henry himself will be excommunicated, and none of the Christian princes of the world will have further dealings with him — except perhaps to invade England on the urgings of the Pope. This is a disaster!'

'It will certainly have long-lasting implications for England's relationships with other nations,' William agreed.

But Eleanor was not to be distracted. 'If the murder of Becket is not to be investigated, this presumably means that you can take no further steps to identify your brother's murderer?'

'Correct, Your Majesty, except that there was more than one man involved, or so I was informed by the sacrist of the monastery at Canterbury. But one — or four — it makes no difference. Were I to begin any investigation, I would be hanged as a traitor, or so I have been warned.'

'That still does not explain why you have chosen to journey here,' Eleanor pointed out.

'I can only say, in my own defence, that it was the first place I thought of, given that the rest of my family are here. I grieve for my brother, and were I to remain in England I would be sorely tempted to risk my neck in searching for his murderers, and perhaps committing a murder or two of my own.'

'You wish to remain here?'

'Nothing would please me more, Your Majesty, and I can perhaps be of service making use of my legal training. I am not sure what laws prevail here in Poitou, but if they are as in England, then I can perhaps put my mind to ensuring that you have an efficient working legal system.'

'You are skilled in drafting legal documents?'

'I am, Your Majesty.'

'How about separation agreements between husband and wife?'

Adele shot William a warning look, and he opted to take the roundabout route.

'It is a common issue here in Poitou?'

Eleanor considered her next words briefly before opting for honesty. 'It could become a real issue here in the Palace of Poitiers. I am not here in my native country because I seek to wallow in childhood memories, William. I am here to escape my husband, for reasons that I care not to elaborate upon. Sooner or later he will leave off cavorting with that Clifford whore and come over here, ordering my return to his bed. I would prefer that we separate on terms that will allow me to remain as the Countess of Poitou, with inheritance rights for my son Richard, and perhaps even the most recent of Henry's offspring, little John. They are both with me here in Poitiers. If I gain my dearest wish they will remain with me, as part of a separation treaty which you can perhaps draw up in anticipation of Henry's arrival, whenever that may prove to be.'

'The other royal children, Your Majesty?' William ventured.

Eleanor grimaced. 'My oldest daughter with Henry — Matilda — is already lost to me by a marriage to which she was condemned by her father's lust for dominance of the north of Europe. Matilda is married to that brute Henry of Saxony, who is old enough to be her father, and no doubt Henry is at present hawking our other two daughters, Eleanor and Joan, among other old men with whom he seeks political alliances against Louis of France. He has already divided up his empire among the sons, and Richard came a very poor last in the shuffle, apart from being betrothed to a princess of France who is little older than your delightful daughter Joan. She shares the nursery with John, who appears destined to inherit nothing at all.'

When negotiating the Treaty of Montmirail almost two years previously, Henry and Louis of France had agreed upon the betrothal of Richard of England to Alys of France, the then nine-year-old daughter of Louis by his second wife, Constance of Castile. The young princess had been taken back to England in the care of Henry and Eleanor, but was now living under Henry's sole wardship in England, even though it had been intended that she would take up her abode in Aquitaine, of which she would one day be countess upon her marriage to Richard.

This was the result of other provisions that Henry had already made regarding his vast inheritance. Young Henry had been proclaimed King of England and Duke of Normandy, while Richard was to receive Aquitaine and Geoffrey was promised Brittany, which technically was not at that time Henry's to bequeath. This left John with nothing.

'You will be seeking more by way of inheritance for Richard and John?' William asked.

Eleanor gave a hollow laugh. 'I may well be negotiating for my continued freedom, should I seek to interfere with Henry's arrangements for disposing of the empire he has been carefully amassing these many years, like a miser with his gold. But it would be a comfort to have someone like yourself available, to warn me of any pitfalls that may exist in any agreement that I may be offered.'

'Are your chambers sufficient to accommodate a husband and boisterous young son?' William asked, grinning at Adele lasciviously.

'Almost certainly not,' replied Eleanor, 'but this castle is large, and somewhat underused of late. There are spacious chambers on the ground floor, the only disagreeable aspect of which is the proximity of the stables. However, they are largely silent at night, when you would most wish peace and quiet. I have no doubt that young Hugh here would welcome being so close to the horses. Can he ride yet?'

'I certainly can!' Hugh replied eagerly. 'And I once shot a boar on the estate — from the saddle!'

It was impossible not to be enchanted by the boy's naive enthusiasm, and everyone round the table chuckled.

'You make up for your skill on horseback by the slowness of your learning,' William reminded him.

'That can easily be remedied with a good tutor,' Eleanor advised them, 'and Richard has the best in the whole of Poitou. He is now fourteen years old, and lacking companions as he labours away at his letters, so he might welcome the addition of young Hugh in the schoolroom. Hopefully they will become as friendly as his sister Joan has become with my youngest son John, who is only three years younger than her. You would mistake them for brother and sister, and one day she will no doubt boast of having chased a prince of England around a nursery, threatening to pull his hair.'

'You are most gracious and generous, my lady,' Adele mumbled through threatening tears.

'Nonsense!' Eleanor replied lightly. 'It is so refreshing to find such a happy family — one that is not constantly at odds, and squabbling over the most absurd and inconsequential matters of detail. Now, if Hugh has eaten enough of that side of meat, I suggest that I call my chamberlain and have him arrange your accommodation. I would that Adele continue to join me each day for dinner, but suppers may be served to your entire family nightly in your own chambers.'

'Do you believe in Christ's great mercy?' Adele asked William as they lay side by side later that night, fully spent after their eager passion.

'I do now,' William panted back. 'But by living a celibate life, he didn't know what he was missing!'

King Henry needed someone to advise him what to do next. Pope Alexander III placed all Henry's estates under interdict and began a very public process designed to lead to Becket being declared a saint as well as a Christian martyr. Henry sent delegates to Rome with suggested peace terms, and was obliged to promise not only to revoke the Constitutions of Clarendon, but also to embark on a Crusade. He took urgent steps to honour the first of those undertakings, while hoping that one of his sons would take up the second, because he had enough to think about without embarking on a journey that might occupy two years and risk his death.

One of those distracting matters was the settlement of Brittany on his twelve-year-old son Geoffrey, who was growing impatient. Henry had acquired authority in that dukedom by first of all coming to the assistance of Duke Conan, then persuading him to name Geoffrey as his heir upon his betrothal to his daughter Constance, who was still only ten years old, but living at the English court. When Conan died that year, and Henry had still not immediately handed Brittany to Geoffrey, or given permission for him to marry his almost infant bride, the young man fell easy prey to his equally discontented older brothers, Young Henry and Richard.

Young Henry had waited long enough, in his mind, to be handed some vestige of kingship other than a hollow title based on a promise. In particular he wanted castles, more money and a greater say in the management of the realm. He was also horrified by the assassination of Becket, and had been advised, by some of those who had been there, that it had occurred on the drunken command of his father. Becket had been Henry's tutor in his earlier years, and he genuinely grieved for the saintly old man who had in some ways been more like a father to him than Henry had. He was easily stirred into rebellion by disaffected and fearful nobles at the court. They reasoned that if King Henry was so dangerously unstable that he was capable, while in his cups, of having an archbishop murdered, then perhaps they might be safer living under the rule of an impressionable young man who they could manipulate.

Seemingly unaware of the pressure building up within his own immediate family, Henry allowed himself to be distracted by the fact that Louis of France now had a male heir, Philip Augustus, by his third wife Adela of Champagne, and had greatly strengthened his alliances by intermarriages between his daughters and Adela's brothers. Henry was in urgent need of further allies through marriage, and he first of all married off his twelve-year-old daughter Eleanor to King Alfonso of Castile, then announced that his youngest son, John, who was still only five, was to be betrothed to Alais of Savoy. This, Henry believed, would result in John acquiring his own estates along the French borders with Italy. However, to make John seem like someone other than a landless adventurer, he also transferred the Normandy castles of Chinon, Loudun and Mirebeau to him, even though, given John's infancy, Henry would continue to control them. This final piece of diplomacy on Henry's part, regarding which he consulted no-one, rapidly blew up in his face.

The first, and most obvious, adverse reaction came from Young Henry, since Normandy had been promised to him, complete with all its fortresses. Already burning with resentment regarding his father's refusal to allow him greater royal autonomy, he searched around for potential allies for a rebellion, and in this he was spoiled for choice. Very soon he had been promised military support by the Kings of Scotland and France and the Counts of Boulogne, Flanders and Blois, and could count on several leading English barons who were genuinely appalled by the fate of Becket, and saw potential advancement for themselves by favouring the new royal generation. A group of disaffected barons also staged uprisings in Brittany, Maine, Angouleme — and Poitou. It was the uprising here, and the failure of Eleanor to take any steps to suppress it, that made Henry suspicious. With the sizeable army that had already crushed the revolt in England, he crossed the Channel.

It was known that Young Henry had reacted to the reversal of fortunes in England by fleeing to Paris, where he was made welcome by Louis VII and formed a firm friendship with his heir apparent Philip Augustus. His father was suspicious that Young Henry might try to recruit the rest of his family in the rebellion, and therefore placed men on the main routes between Paris and Poitiers to intercept any potential messengers between Paris and his remaining sons Geoffrey, Richard and John. They were all known to be enjoying their mother's hospitality in the capital city of Poitou, while doing nothing about the uprising in neighbouring Brittany.

Henry's efforts were soon rewarded, when messengers were intercepted carrying despatches from Young Henry to his younger brothers, urging them to join him in Paris, where they would be guaranteed a warm welcome and an opportunity to renegotiate their future inheritances from a position of military superiority. Rather than journeying immediately to confront Eleanor and her remaining sons, Henry had the original messengers done to death, replaced them with trusted men of his own, and instructed them to deliver the messages. He then waited at Rouen to see what Eleanor would do.

A month later his worst suspicions were confirmed, when word reached him that a large party that included Eleanor, Richard, John, Geoffrey and various royal servants had left Poitiers and were heading for Paris.

The trap had been sprung, and Henry's rage was almost ungovernable.

XIV

The past few years had seemed to flow like a pleasant dream, as William and Adele settled into their new set of chambers in the balmy atmosphere of south-western France, with its gentle Atlantic breezes and mild winters. Adele's duties were never onerous, since Queen Eleanor seemed content to watch her three younger sons develop into young men, and never once allowed herself to be drawn into any of the baronial squabbles in which her subjects seemed to be permanently engaged. Nor was she troubled by any visits from King Henry, since his hands were tied by the horrified reaction to the death of Becket. The late archbishop's final resting place had now become a place of pilgrimage, and his tomb was rumoured to work miracles.

As they all began to enjoy the milder breezes that blew around the palace ramparts in the spring of 1174, Adele was delighted to advise Eleanor that she was once again expecting, and would need to be temporarily relieved of her admittedly light duties once the autumn months closed in on them again.

They had no reason to be apprehensive of bringing another child into the comfortable world that they occupied. Hugh and Joan were certainly enjoying the privileges of a palace upbringing, without any of the burdens that royalty normally imposed. They had each found a friend, given that children of all ages, nationalities, languages and religions will form natural bonds without any concern for the differences that, in later life, may set them apart.

Twelve-year-old Hugh had quickly found a natural mentor in fourteen-year-old Richard, and had applied himself ardently to the study of Latin, Greek, music and mathematics in which Richard had been engaged since he had first been consigned to a tutor.

Such was Hugh's determination to be accepted by the older boy that he made strenuous efforts to rival him in learning. His quick and enquiring brain ensured that by the end of the first year, it was the older Richard who looked to his young schoolroom companion to assist him in more difficult passages of translation, or the declension of Latin verbs. He was able to repay the eager boy by taking him as a companion into the tiltyard that had been constructed on the lower castle greensward, where Armand Betelier, the Captain of the Poitiers Palace Guard, was charged with the duty of ensuring that the heir to Aquitaine and Poitou would grow into a skilled warrior.

Armand rapidly realised that the sturdy and determined English boy had a natural instinct for hand-to-hand combat. Despite the disparity in the sizes of the two boys, he was able to make use of Hugh's superior skill with weapons in order to provide a ready opponent for Richard as they slashed, parried, thrust and hacked at each other with blunted blades. Likewise when it came to horsemanship; although Hugh's experience had been restricted to heavier farm beasts, he had learned how to control a horse fifteen times his bodyweight, and took naturally to the coursers that he and Richard were taught to mount and dismount at speed, then guide through a tricky series of obstacles placed in their path inside the inner bailey.

There was a similar growing rapport between Richard's younger brother John and Hugh's younger sister Joan, who shared a nursery. John was hardly at an age to appreciate that one day he might be the king of one of the largest dynastic empires in the Christian world, whereas the cheeky, precocious girl who shared his toys was merely the offspring of a lady in waiting of his mother's. For her part, Joan saw John simply as a younger boy who she could tease, chase around the nursery, torment and tickle, and it reached the stage at which their frustrated nursery governess could not persuade either of them to do something without allowing the other to join in. She secretly confided in Queen Eleanor that given the way things were developing between them, if Her Majesty was looking for a suitable bride for her youngest son, she need look no further than the nursery.

Even though they all seemed safe enough behind the walls of Poitiers Palace, the happy parents of the newborn boy, christened Robert, were conscious that they would be pushing Eleanor's generosity to the limit by asking for yet another non-noble to be raised among royal princes. They were also uneasily aware that they had not shown their faces on the Repton estate for some years, and that it was important for the steward to be reminded daily that although he did such a commendable job of running the estate, it was not his.

With a heavy heart, and with Adele's sobs still ringing in his ears for the first few days of his lonely trek north, William — with only an elderly widowed nurse for company — took one-year-old Robert across the Channel in a pannier slung to the side of his horse that doubled as a crib during their overnight stays. Three weeks later, he charged Steward Thomas Derby with the solemn duty of supervising Robert's upbringing, with a view to his running the estate for the family when he came of age. Then, after leaving the nurse with many heartfelt thanks and a bag of gold coins, William pointed his mount back south.

He had been back at Poitiers barely a few months before they received the first of the messages from Young Henry, and became entangled in events that disrupted all their lives.

Eleanor and Adele were seated quietly on padded chairs on either side of the cheerfully blazing fire that had been lit to combat the chill of early spring, each engaged in needlecraft, when William was admitted. Adele looked up with a warm smile, then saw the solemn look on his face and felt a frisson of apprehension.

'What is it, my dear?' she enquired, as usual ignoring the protocol under which Eleanor should have been the first to speak. Eleanor put down the hand-embroidered altar cloth on which she had been working as she raised her eyebrows.

William sighed and brought a lengthy vellum into sight from behind his back. 'It comes from your son Henry, madam. The seal was royal, and it was unbroken. I took the liberty of breaking it, and it is perhaps as well that I did, for I must caution you against its contents.'

'More complaints regarding his father's parsimony?'

'It has gone way beyond that, my lady,' William said solemnly. 'It would seem that he put himself at the head of that latest uprising in England, and was then obliged to seek sanctuary in Paris. Indeed, on reflection I suspect that he was its instigator, and that it owed nothing to the unjust death of Archbishop Becket.'

'Henry will no doubt react with one of his red angers, and begin breaking more furniture in his rage,' Eleanor replied with a slight shudder. 'Thanks be to God that I no longer have to witness those.'

'You may do if you answer Young Henry's call, and then fail, my lady.'

'Your meaning?'

'He requests that you bring the princes Richard, Geoffrey and John and join him in Paris. He claims to have the support of Louis of France, not to mention the King of Scotland and numerous French counts and dukes. His plan is to become King of England immediately with their assistance.'

'Does he say what he intends to do with his father?'

'Not in so many words, but clearly he is betraying him at a time when he must be the most unpopular monarch in Europe. But I would counsel against accepting his invitation.'

'Why, pray?' Eleanor asked, the light in her eyes suggesting that she would relish a change of scene.

William took the proffered seat and explained. 'For one, it may be a trap, designed to test your loyalty. The seal was the general palace one employed on all official royal documents, and many have access to it. We cannot be certain that this was written at Henry's request, and indeed we must not assume that, in his exile, Young Henry had access to it.'

'Does it bear a signature?' Eleanor asked, and William nodded as he handed it over. She glanced only briefly at it. 'This is indeed Henry's own clumsy hand. What is your other objection?'

William coughed politely, then explained. 'With the greatest of respect to your royal person, you are hardly well placed to bring an army into the field. The young Richard is barely a man, and as for John, well, even my daughter can best him in a tumble across the carpet. Geoffrey seems more dedicated to pretended warfare in the tourney than in reality on the battlefield. The only reason why the Young Henry might wish to welcome you to Paris is to rub your husband's nose further into the dirt. It would also give his uprising the vestige of authority if even the Queen of England is content to become its former queen.'

'I hear what you say, and I respect the wisdom of your advice,' Eleanor replied calmly as she put her needlework down on the table to her side. 'But I cannot ignore a request for a meeting with my firstborn. Well, second-born, but the oldest surviving of my brood. As for rubbing Henry's nose in dirt, he is quite capable of finding his own pile of it and breathing in. I do not scruple against making him reveal how friendless he has become.'

'But the risk of a trap, madam?'

'My own son would not lead me into a trap, William. The seal was, you say, unbroken, and the signature was his. We will leave by the end of the week — please make the necessary arrangements with the chamberlain and the Captain of the Guard.'

'We are to accompany you, my lady?' Adele enquired.

Eleanor nodded. 'I cannot imagine being in Paris without looking my best. Only you seem to have mastered the sorcery of making me appear to be still only thirty years of age, as I was when I foolishly fell for a gallant young adventurer who turned into a fat, bad-tempered, old despot. So, let us waste no more time about it.'

'But, madam…' William began. He was stopped by Eleanor's frosty stare.

'I said *now*, William, unless you missed my meaning.'

They got as far as Authon-du-Perche, a small village on the road between Le Mans and Chartres, where they could no longer claim to have been heading for Rouen or Caen, but were clearly bound for Paris. The road ahead was heavily wooded, and as the modest progress of horses, wagons, litters and outriders passed under the shade of a line of native pines, a group of at least twenty heavily armed knights rode sedately out of the shade on either side of the road ahead of them. They were wearing the familiar Plantagenet livery of gold lions on a red background that Henry had long since made the official blazon of England, and their leader announced that they were to halt on the order of King Henry of England.

William looked behind him, to where at least another dozen men at arms, similarly clad, had drawn up. He called out in a low voice that unless they wished to see their modest armed retinue of less than ten hacked down by a vastly superior force, they should do as they were told.

'Why don't we take them on?' Hugh enquired eagerly from his mount immediately behind his father's.

'Don't be an idiot,' Richard muttered from alongside him. 'We're hopelessly outnumbered. We just have to enquire what they want of us.'

'They're wearing royal blazons,' William muttered from the corner of his mouth, 'so presumably your father has sent them to intercept us.'

That point was left in no doubt when the leader of the royal party nudged his horse into a slow walk down the procession, then lifted the curtain that was obscuring the interior of the ornate litter from sight. He gave a sarcastic half bow to Eleanor from his saddle.

'His Majesty King Henry requests the pleasure of your company at Rouen, being mindful of the danger you would be incurring were you to remain on the road to Paris. His continued regard for your safety also led him to order me to guard your person all the way. Those who accompany you will also be obliged to continue to do so. Let us lose no time, since we are expected at the castle at Alencon by nightfall.'

This proved to be the first of three castles at which they were all lodged overnight, securely guarded by men at arms who had no respect for the modesty of the women in the group. They threatened to slit the throats of the men who protested that the ladies should be allowed their own chambers, and not be expected to bed down with the rest of the party on straw pallets in the main hall of each of their temporary prisons. It was almost a relief, four days later, to see the spires of Rouen ahead, until they remembered that they were not about to be welcomed as honoured guests.

Once they had been ordered off their horses, and Eleanor had been assisted, somewhat brusquely, from her litter, they were taken inside the mighty castle that held such mixed memories for the lady who was still officially the Duchess of Normandy. She, along with Adele — and William, at his insistence — were led into a modest ground-floor chamber in which they were served a very meagre meal of bread and meat, washed down with an inferior wine that was probably drawn from the kitchen. Then they sat and waited.

It was dark before the chamber door was kicked open by an angry riding boot. There in the doorway stood a red-faced King Henry, his heavy breathing betraying the fact that he had just returned from the hunt. He looked disdainfully at Eleanor and Adele, then his gaze shifted to William, and he gave a snarl.

'The runaway Clerk of Justiciary, unless my memory plays me false! We wondered where you had slunk off to, although we did not care unduly.'

'I had a yearning to see my wife and daughter, since my twin brother died in the defence of the Archbishop of Canterbury, and I was somewhat lacking in family,' William replied haughtily.

Henry's face went red as he spat on the carpet and ordered him to remain silent. Then he diverted his eyes to Eleanor and sneered. 'That was, of course, not the only intended family reunion, was it? All four of my rebellious sons enjoying the hospitality of your former husband in Paris, plotting against my throne — is this how you planned to repay my generosity?'

'No — it's how I repay your infidelity,' Eleanor replied with a look of contempt. 'How goes the Clifford whore?'

'She goes better than you, anyway,' Henry chortled. 'Like a barn door in a gale, since you ask. But she is back in England, so you need not concern yourself about her. What *should* concern you is how you will employ your time while you remain my prisoner here in Rouen.'

'Will I be allowed my attendant, Adele here?'

'Why not, since she is the only companion you *will* be allowed.'

'And her husband?' William enquired. 'Or do you intend to drag me back to England for an execution?'

Adele gave a whimper of fear, which Henry seemed to appreciate, given the smirk on his face as he looked back at William. 'Give me one good reason why you should not hang here at Rouen, rather than incur the expense of carting you back across the Channel.'

'What I know regarding the circumstances of Becket's death,' William replied calmly. 'While I am alive I can, should you wish, advise the rest of Christendom that the four men who took the life of the archbishop made no claim to be acting on your behalf, or at your bidding.'

'You know that for a fact?' Henry enquired eagerly.

'I travelled to Canterbury when I learned that my brother had also been slain, and the sacrist from the monastery gave me a very detailed — and very distressing — account of what transpired.'

'Then why should I not get that same public proclamation directly from him, rather than acquire it second-hand from you?'

'Because he is hardly well disposed towards you, and will claim sanctuary if you send men in search of him. Not that sanctuary seemed to be of any protection to poor old Tom Becket. But I was, at the time, one of the justiciar's staff, and therefore my account of events would be the more believable, even though I would imagine that I have been stripped of my position.'

'You are also stripped of the estate that I granted you, ingrate that you are,' Henry told him heatedly. 'But I may still find a use for you. I am advised that two of your children — a boy and a girl — have become companions to my two, Richard and John. Is that correct?'

'It is, but why?'

'Because both sons have insisted that they be allowed to remain with them when we journey back to England. I have hopes that Richard and John will soon come to realise how badly they were misled by their older brother Henry, and I wish them to remain happily with me, as far away from their pernicious mother as possible. They will feel her absence less if they have close companions. And they will act as perfect hostages to your future loyalty in your new duties.'

'What duties are they?' William asked.

Henry smiled sadistically. 'Since your wife will attend upon Eleanor, it is fitting that you become her gaoler, answerable to me. If she escapes, or becomes once again involved in plots against my throne, you will have even less family. Do I make my meaning clear?'

'Perfectly,' William muttered.

'Very well, then,' Henry smiled further as he lifted one foot from the ground in order to deliver a loud fart. 'I leave you with that warning, and that lingering smell.'

'He was ever a pig,' Eleanor remarked as she wrinkled her nose. 'But that could have been worse, I suppose.'

'You mean because he let us live?' Adele asked.

Eleanor shook her head. 'No — I meant that he *could* have been eating fish.'

Events rapidly accelerated, and the first sign that Henry was seeking to centralise all control in his own hands, while failing in his judgment, was the transfer of his prisoners from Rouen across the Channel to Winchester. Travelling with Eleanor, Adele and William was Margaret of France, who had now been married to the Young Henry for over ten years. It was widely believed that Henry was holding her hostage against Young Henry's return. It had the desired effect.

Young Henry sent several French clergymen to negotiate a safe return to England, and the following Easter he wept on his father's shoulder as the two were briefly reconciled for long enough for Henry to be reinstated as the heir apparent to England and Normandy. This merely incensed the next two sons in line, Geoffrey and Richard. They had still not been allowed any power in their respective lands of Brittany and Aquitaine, and were fobbed off with half the revenues from the estates that did homage to them in name only. They had been released in Rouen, and allowed to go their separate ways, after assuring their father that they had unwisely allowed themselves to be seduced by Henry's promise of rich estates once he was king, but had now seen the error of their ways. Neither of them could quite believe that their father, so merciless towards others, was so naive and trusting so far as they were concerned. They had no intention of remaining loyal.

Richard in particular had another grievance festering that involved more than just land, and had the potential to make him a laughing stock throughout Europe. The Treaty of Montmirail had contained a provision under which Richard became betrothed to Alys of France, Louis' daughter. Her dowry was the County of Berry, on one of Aquitaine's borders and of strategic importance to Henry, who had been granted Alys's wardship under an arrangement whereby she was intended to reside in Aquitaine under the supervision of Eleanor.

Alys had been quietly coming of marriageable age, and developing a beauty that most men found breath-taking, when Eleanor, Geoffrey, Richard and John had been captured on their way to join Young Henry at Louis' Court. Rather than leave Alys alone, and exposed, across the Channel, King Henry made arrangements for her to join the party that landed in England. Whereas Alys's former chaperone Eleanor was confined within a grim set of chambers in Winchester, Alys was taken down to a castle in Devizes, Wiltshire, in circumstances that grew increasingly ominous when Rosamund Clifford died. It soon became rumoured that King Henry had made Alys his mistress.

Richard was incensed, and confronted his father late one evening in Westminster Palace. 'Why do you humiliate me in this fashion?' he demanded.

Henry gave him a steely glare. 'Why do *you* accept idle rumours concocted against me by those who wish me ill?'

'If you truly do not have young Alys in your bed nightly, then why do you not let me marry her, as was the intention all along? She is now of marriageable age, and most comely, but you keep her from me, thereby promoting the rumours that you have made her your mistress. You have finally allowed

Geoffrey to marry Constance, and he is Duke of Brittany. So why do you hold back — is it because you do not wish me to acquire the dowry lands of Berry, or because you want her body for yourself?'

'I will take no more insult from you!' Henry yelled as his face flushed red. 'I get more respect from your younger brother, and I am minded to give him Ireland.'

'Oh yes — *dear* John!' Richard all but spat contemptuously. 'Your precious lapdog with his constant companion young Joan, the daughter of the man who acts as my mother's jailor. She is only just approaching womanhood, but no doubt John has had her already. Or is he saving her for you — is that why he is so favoured?'

'Enough!' Henry bellowed. 'You will leave my sight this instant, and take yourself off somewhere of use to me, if you wish to retain my favour. You might begin with Aquitaine, whose nobles have become fractious since your mother was removed from Poitiers. Go over there and prove yourself worthy of the name of Plantagenet.'

'And if I use that opportunity to join forces with my brother Henry, given that I am more highly regarded in the French court than I am in the court of my own father?'

'Then you will *never* wed Alys!' Henry threatened, adding, with a sneer, 'I may well be doing her a great service by preserving her from marriage with you anyway. Were I to believe rumours concerning you with the ease that you do those regarding me, then I would conclude that your relationship with the French heir Philip Augustus is not as God intended.'

'A vile accusation!' Richard yelled as his face reddened. 'I do not deny that we became close friends after you introduced us — mainly because you were seeking yet another peace treaty with his father — but there is nothing more to that relationship.'

'Then go away and prove your manhood,' Henry taunted him. 'Begin in Aquitaine, and when you have silenced the querulous nobles who are demanding your wicked mother's return, *then* we might consider if you are man enough for matrimony. Now, get out of my sight!'

Richard stormed out of the Audience Chamber and returned to his own apartments, where he advised a startled Hugh Repton that they were leaving for Aquitaine. 'You need not bother seeking your father's permission, since fathers are not to be trusted.'

XV

'I miss the children,' Adele whispered with a long sigh as she lay with her head on William's chest. 'In some ways, that's the worst part of being imprisoned here for so long. Hugh has been taken away by Richard, who's likely to be involving him in real fighting now that the nation has risen against King Henry yet again, and as for poor Joan, well, I dread to think what fate might befall her at Westminster. We haven't seen her for so long, but I hear tell from some of the kitchen staff transferred from London that she's grown into a beautiful young woman, and that John would hardly let her alone until his father intervened. I just hope he doesn't take her off to Ireland with him.'

She had previously had good cause to be concerned for Joan's welfare. Prince John, once he'd reached the age of fifteen, had begun to display most of his father's bad traits without any of his redeeming features. He had an unhealthy interest in his former nursery companion Joan, who was by then a well-developed eighteen-year-old. She had complained to their governess about his unwelcome hands feeling her body, and occasionally finding their way under her gown, and the governess in turn had quietly advised the king. After chuckling, King Henry had sent John across the Irish Sea to deal with the fractious Irish rebels who refused to accept English sovereignty.

Joan had then been transferred to the pool of ladies who had been raised and trained to wait upon a queen who was now imprisoned in Winchester. The ladies now constituted a sort of harem from which the young nobles seeking to remain in Henry's favour selected brides.

Henry had two reasons for taking this action, neither of which had anything to do with concern for Joan's welfare. For one thing, if she had been more seriously mistreated by John, then her father William would have less reason to closely guard Queen Eleanor, since Henry's threat against her would have become an empty one. But, far more importantly, Henry appointed himself as Joan's guardian and could now set about looking for a suitable match for her among those young nobles who would be duly grateful to him for permitting them to marry such a comely young bride. When they eventually learned of Joan's entry into 'the henhouse', as it was commonly known, William and Adele exchanged one concern for another, but at least they knew that she was still alive and enjoying more luxurious surroundings than theirs.

As for their son Hugh, William was apprehensive of what future might be awaiting him as the constant companion of Prince Richard, given the dangers of the battlefield. He and Adele regularly sought news of what might be happening in Aquitaine and Poitiers, where Richard was believed to be suppressing local rebellions in his father's name.

Their most immediate concern was for their youngest, Robert, who was trapped on an estate that his parents no longer possessed. Had he been cast out by agents of King Henry, assuming that his presence at Repton was known, or was he still residing there, ignorant of his true origins? There came a day when William could no longer bear to hear Adele's gentle sobs at night when she believed him to be asleep. After obtaining Eleanor's consent, and making elaborate arrangements to conceal his temporary absence, William rode north.

On his approach to the Repton manor house door, he was met by a sturdy young man who stepped out into the yard with a worried expression. William recognised him as the adult version of the boy who had played with their eldest son Hugh all those years ago, and he called out, 'It's Thomas, isn't it?'

'Aye, that's me,' Thomas confirmed, 'an' yer face is familiar, but it's bin some years now. Yer doesn't own this estate anymore, does yer?'

'No, I don't,' William admitted. 'I heard that it had been given to the Church, but I'm not here to reclaim it or anything — I just need to learn of the fate of the small baby I left here seven years ago, along with a nurse.'

Thomas smiled reassuringly. 'As fer young Robert, yer'll find 'im in the top field, fellin' trees wiv me eldest boy Peter. I'm afraid we 'ad ter bring 'im up as one've our own, me an' Meg, after that there nurse got 'erself waylaid an' robbed ter death when she spent the gold yer give 'er too freely down the Black Swan. I 'opes yer don't mind, but we 'ad no option, an' the lad's turned out well enough.'

'No, I'm very, *very* grateful,' William all but laughed with relief. 'It means that King Henry will never learn his true identity, and he'll be safe here. Is your father still the steward?'

'Nah,' Thomas replied sadly. "E were took from us by an ague when 'is old bones was approachin' seventy years've age. The priory at Lenton what owns the place now was content ter let me run things, an' it's now one've the richest estates this side've Nottin'um.'

'So it's no hardship for you to continue to raise Robert?'

'Why would it be? Like I said, the estate's doin' fine, an' we've got three more've our own anyway, so Robert's got brothers an' sisters that 'e seems ter get on wiv. So yer doesn't need ter worry none. D'yer want me ter show yer up ter the top field, so's you can see 'im fer yerself?'

William choked back a tear as he shook his head. 'It's perhaps best for both of us if I don't. I can just reassure his mother that he's come to no harm.'

'In these dangerous times, that's a blessin' in itself,' Thomas agreed, 'an' I promise yer that 'e'll be safe enough 'ere. I'll teach 'im all I knows about runnin' an estate, and then one day 'e can manage one've 'is own fer some master or other.'

After thanking the man profusely, and insisting that he accept the small bag of gold coins, William rode back with a sad heart, albeit reassured that his youngest would survive.

He also reflected on how history had a habit of repeating itself. He and Alain had grown up as virtual orphans — in their case inside a monastery — with very occasional visits from a man claiming to be their uncle, and never knowing their parents. And now Robert — the son of a leading royal adviser and a lady in waiting to a queen — was to be raised completely ignorant of his origins, leading the simple life of an estate worker, believing its steward and his wife to be his parents. This was the best outcome he could have hoped for, and any tears he felt like shedding for the loss of a son were just self-indulgence on his part. One had to adjust to the turbulent times created by the bickering of the royal brood.

But the uprisings that continued to challenge King Henry were not confined to his immediate household, and by 1182 he was surrounded by enemies. Most of those were of the old variety — barons anxious to increase their power and influence by playing off one royal son after another against their increasingly irascible father, in the hope that by rallying to the cause of a rebel prince they might become leading nobles of a future King of England. But there were also discontented lords in lands across the Channel, most notably Normandy, the Vexin, Anjou and Blois, who chafed under an English yoke and looked to France, now ruled by the young Philip Augustus, to restore them to their former power. Finally there was the lingering stigma of the murder of Becket, which meant that King Henry could not look for any support from either the Pope or the English Church. This was perhaps something that he *could* redress.

But by the time that he did, England was in as big a state of chaos as it had been during the final years of Stephen's reign. King Henry was drawn back into Normandy by what appeared to be a co-ordinated uprising by his vassals in the Vexin led by the fickle de Montforts. While he was heading for his southern Normandy borders, King William of Scotland took the opportunity to launch a massive attack on both sides of the northern border, taking strategic castles in Cumbria and Northumbria.

William and Adele, effectively imprisoned behind the walls of Winchester with the queen they were officially guarding, heard only brief accounts of what was transpiring elsewhere. Only Eleanor seemed to take any satisfaction from what she heard.

'Henry is finally reaping his reward for the many evil deeds he has done,' she remarked gloatingly as yet more news was delivered of the steady southerly progress of William of Scotland through the northern counties. 'He has not a friend left in the world, and even his own sons have turned their backs on him. Young Henry is with Philip Augustus in Paris, no doubt preparing to sack the whole of Normandy, while Richard is back in his beloved Aquitaine, from where he can attack his father's army from the west. Meanwhile, our long-standing enemies in Scotland find the nation wide open to them. I wonder what King William will do with me when he finally reaches Winchester.'

Late one spring afternoon, as the three of them sat glumly watching yet another heavy rain shower darken the walls of the tower across the courtyard, an usher poked his head around the door and announced that they had a visitor. As usual his manner was blunt, gruff and disrespectful, and he did not enquire whether or not they wished their visitor to be admitted. A tall man strode in with a broad smile, and Adele gave a cry of recognition as she leapt to her feet and welcomed him with a warm hug.

'You remember my brother Hugh, of course — the Earl of Chester?' she asked eagerly.

William nodded as he recalled the triple matrimonial event in Evreux that had included his betrothal to Adele, along with that of her half-brother Hugh to a daughter of de Montfort. Hugh no longer looked like the fresh-faced boy that he had been then; his face was lined by stress, and his hair was greying at the temples. 'So what brings you here?' William enquired suspiciously.

Hugh gave him a smile that was so obviously false that William almost laughed. 'Why should a man not visit his own sister?' Hugh asked.

'Once in all these years?' William challenged. 'What sort of brotherly concern is that? And where were you when Henry imprisoned us all in the first place?'

'Does anyone mind if I ask a question?' Eleanor interrupted sarcastically. 'In case no-one gets around to the introductions during all this family jollity, I used to be the Queen of England. My question is how things fare in the north.'

'Apologies, Your Majesty,' Hugh replied with a red-faced bow. 'It is because of how things fare in the north that I am here today.'

'So *not* just to visit me?' Adele responded with a mock pout.

Hugh shook his head. 'That is indeed the pretence under which I ventured here, but I have another reason.'

'You *do* surprise me,' William replied with a sneer.

'I am here to arrange your release — all of you, of course, but primarily Queen Eleanor,' explained Hugh.

'You said "arrange",' William pointed out. 'Not "secure"?'

'Not yet. That will come later. But you must prepare yourselves for travel in a matter of days.'

'From one prison to another?' Eleanor asked sceptically.

Hugh shook his head. 'From here to Poitiers, Your Majesty.'

'God grant that you are not joking at our expense!' Eleanor gasped as she raised a hand to her mouth. 'You come at the command of my son Richard?'

'In his cause, anyway,' Hugh agreed. 'It is a long story.'

'And we have at least an hour to spare before they serve our evening pigswill, so pray enlighten us,' William requested. 'But first have a mug of this coloured water to grease your throat — that's about all it's fit for.'

Hugh took a long draught of what passed for wine, then took a seat and explained. 'I have already lost half my fortresses to William of Scotland, but for some reason he held back at the walls of Lancaster, behind which I was hidden in the expectation of capture. He then sent me a message to the effect that he would cease his southerly progress if I would secure your release. He has seemingly been promised the whole of England north of the Trent once King Henry has been overthrown, but has also been charged with the task of having Queen Eleanor released into the custody of her son Richard.'

'So Richard is behind this?' Eleanor beamed. 'He was ever my favourite, and he loves his mother.' She wiped away a stray tear.

Hugh shook his head. 'His was not the original order, it seems. So far as I can tell, it comes from Philip Augustus of France, who sets great store by having you released, if only to distract King Henry even more.'

'I doubt that my so-called husband gives a fig for me anymore.'

'I should perhaps add, in the interest of completeness,' Hugh went on, 'that I did not receive this information other than by the hand of King William's messenger. However, I was approached with the same request by my wife's family — the de Montforts, who have reasons of their own for wishing to divert Henry from his current march on the Vexin. I am also advised that Philip of Flanders plans an invasion by way of Norwich, to drag Henry back to England while the combined forces of France and Aquitaine overrun Normandy and Anjou.'

'It sounds as if this has been well prepared,' William muttered. 'But is it being mooted that we break out of here with an armed force under your command?'

'Would that I *had* such a force,' Hugh replied ruefully. 'Most of them have been lost to me in attempting to hold back William of Scotland, while King Henry plays at being the next Charlemagne across the Channel.'

'Then how?' was William's next question.

'Written orders from the Justiciar of England. Well, one of them at least. Perhaps you can guess which one?'

William thought for a moment. 'Yours is not the only family connected to the de Montforts. Was not the young Simon affianced to a daughter of Leicester?'

'Correct,' Hugh confirmed. 'Amicia, daughter of de Beaumont, Earl of Leicester, and now the Lady of Evreux and Montfort-l'Amaury, has prevailed upon Leicester to sign the necessary release papers.'

'Wonderful!' Eleanor enthused. 'Henry's friends are deserting him like rats from a grain store that has caught fire!'

But William still wasn't convinced. 'I know de Beaumont to be a loyal servant of King Henry. I cannot believe that he would betray him at this moment, when England is about to fall to Scotland. And if it comes to that, my lord of Chester, what becomes of your wealth and position when and if everything north of the Trent becomes part of Scotland, with no doubt a border at Nottingham?'

'I get to rule most of southern England,' Hugh smiled. 'The loser will then be de Beaumont.'

'And he has agreed to sign for our release, knowing this?' William asked in disbelief.

'He is not aware of the broader plan of escape, thinking only that you are to be transferred to Bristol. When it is revealed that his error led to your escape, Henry will no doubt have his head, but it is the price he must pay for the many years in which his family has sought to hold back mine.'

'I do not believe this man to be genuine, Your Majesty!' William announced sharply. 'I believe him to have been sent by your husband to trick us into a false plot for your escape that would then entitle King Henry to have us executed.'

'You would accuse my own brother of such falsehood?' Adele demanded angrily.

Eleanor held up her hand for silence. 'I am the one who is to be rescued. Were it not for your prior service to me, you would not now be included in this longed-for release.'

'Were it not for our service to you, we would not be here in the first place!' William retorted.

Adele turned bright red. 'Forgive him, Your Majesty — he only speaks what he believes to be the truth!'

'And it *is* of course the truth,' Eleanor conceded. 'But I will not reject this opportunity to be freed from this cesspit of a place and be reunited with my son. If Henry wishes me dead, he could no doubt invent a better excuse for it. We will go along with whatever the gallant Earl of Chester proposes.'

'I shall return here as soon as I have the necessary document from de Beaumont, and we shall ride west as if intended for Bristol,' said Hugh. 'But when we reach Salisbury we shall turn south for Portsmouth, where a vessel will carry you across the Channel, then around the coast of Brittany to La Rochelle, where you will be met by Prince Richard and conveyed to the safety of Poitiers.'

'If Richard is defending Poitou and Aquitaine in Henry's name, as he is claiming to do,' said William, 'then why would he be willing to harbour Queen Eleanor?'

'Your children clearly do not demonstrate the same love for you as Richard does for me,' Eleanor preened. 'We should begin our discreet packing without delay.'

'Talking of children,' William objected, 'you forget our daughter Joan. If I break my promise to King Henry to hold you secure here, then he will take his revenge upon her in a manner that I dare not even begin to contemplate.'

Adele smothered a squeal of fear, and Hugh nodded.

'You refer, of course, to my beautiful niece, and I have already made provision for her. Under pretence that she has need to travel here in order to seek your approval for marriage to a knight from Henry's now deserted court in London, I have arranged for them to accompany us when we bring your transfer papers.'

'You appear to have thought of everything,' William observed in a voice dripping with cynicism. 'Clearly you have convinced Her Majesty, but I shall not acknowledge your service to us — and that of the Earl of Leicester — until we are safely back in Poitiers.'

XVI

Just over a week later they were waiting eagerly in the Great Hall, their baggage surrounding them on the floor, as Hugh of Chester's arrival was announced. For the sake of appearances, he swept in with four men at arms and announced that on the order of Robert de Beaumont, Earl of Leicester, they were being transferred to more secure custody in Bristol.

'But in order that the entire group may be in the one place, I have also been instructed to bring with me Mistress Joan Walsingham, who has been delivered here under the personal protection of Ralph de Coutances.'

Adele gave a shriek of joy as a sheepish face appeared from behind a tall young knight. Then a beautiful young lady came into view, dressed from head to foot in the latest courtly fashion, with long, light auburn tresses that shone in the mid-morning sun. Joan ran to her mother and wrapped herself in her arms as they both sobbed, then transferred her grip to her eagerly waiting father with more tears and exclamations of happiness. Eventually she was composed enough to step back and indicate the imposing young man who had escorted her from Westminster.

'This is Ralph de Coutances, younger brother of the recently consecrated Bishop of Lincoln. He wishes my hand in marriage.'

'And he shall have it, when he proves himself worthy,' William smiled. 'For the time being, he may join our party as we journey from here, in order that we may get to know him better.'

'And it would be best if we lost no further time,' Hugh of Chester urged them. 'I shall get my men to take out your baggage to the wagons we have brought for that purpose.'

'Before we move a foot,' William insisted, 'let me see the signed order from de Beaumont, in order to satisfy myself that this is not some trick.'

Hugh reached inside his cloak and extracted a single sheet of vellum, suitably sealed, which he handed over for William's scrutiny. Instead of handing it back, William called for one of his most trusted men at arms from the small garrison at Winchester and handed it to him.

'Philip, ride hard to Portsmouth with this securely about your person, and await us by the northern town gate. If we have not arrived within the week, ride hard to London and see that it is handed to Justiciar de Lucy, with instruction from me that de Beaumont transferred Queen Eleanor to Bristol without King Henry's authority. That should be enough to remove his head.'

'You are one of the least trusting men I have ever met,' Hugh complained.

William nodded. 'That is why I have survived to be over fifty years of age. It is not that I do not trust you — rather I fear that you have become too gullible in your hunger to see Leicester ruined, and yourself enfeoffed of the southern half of England by a grateful Young Henry. Now, let us depart and see what transpires.'

They inevitably travelled slowly along the well-worn track to Salisbury, made muddy by late spring rain, given that they had two litters and three baggage wagons piled high with clothing and other personal items. Hugh of Chester rode with William at the head of the progress, while men at arms from both Chester's entourage and those drawn from Winchester rode down the side and to the rear. The Bishop of Salisbury was more than content to act as their host for their first night's rest, given that one of their number was the Queen of England, and that the Earl of Chester assured him that he was acting on the orders of the Justiciar of England in escorting the party to Bristol. The following morning, shortly after first light, they struck south towards Portsmouth.

Late on the afternoon of that second day, with salt air in their nostrils as they looked down a long, sloping hill towards the sails in Southampton Water, a large force of men rode out from a side road at a crossing. There were at least fifty of them, all heavily armed. At their head was a middle-aged man with a military bearing and a broad grin that was only too familiar to William, who turned to mutter to Hugh of Chester, 'I tried to warn you.'

Hugh swore profusely as he too recognised the man whose retinue was blocking their progress. 'Leicester, the double-dealing bastard! We are betrayed!'

'Only by your lack of foresight,' William advised him. 'Fortunately, I have played this game for many years, so leave the mutual exchange of unpleasantries to me.'

De Beaumont's grin turned to a sneer as he recognised William. 'The treacherous and long-absent William Walsingham, unless I am mistaken. I had learned that King Henry left you in charge of Eleanor, despite my advice that you were not to be trusted. Now I am proved right — you were heading for Portsmouth, were you not?'

'Where we are heading is none of your business,' came a stern voice from the litter. Eleanor had pulled back the curtain. 'And it's *Queen* Eleanor to you, de Beaumont, so have a mind to your manners.'

'You will need all that arrogance when King Henry has you consigned to a nunnery,' de Beaumont spat back. 'As for the rest of you, a hangman awaits you all, particularly the alleged Earl of Chester.'

'At least you'll be in good company on the gallows,' William replied defiantly, but de Beaumont shook his head.

'I will be richly rewarded for betraying your true colours — all of you. You were fleeing the country, no doubt intent on stirring more rebellion in Aquitaine and Poitou. By leaving Winchester without the king's permission, you are all guilty of treason.'

'And upon whose written order was that made possible?' William enquired with a smirk of his own.

'Mine, clearly, but that was a carefully laid plot of my own devising,' de Beaumont replied. 'I had word that Chester was planning to free *Queen* Eleanor, and I simply played the game when he unwisely sought to involve me in his treasonous scheme. I shall of course deny ever having issued the release order, so that it will look as if Chester freed you on his own authority.'

'How can you hope to deny the authenticity of a document under your own seal?' William enquired with a triumphant grin, to which de Beaumont responded with a sadistic grin of his own.

'You will of course be required to hand back that document, under pain of torture or worse. Once it is destroyed, all evidence of my alleged involvement will be erased, and I shall be rewarded as the person who learned of your escape, and headed you off ere you could reach Portsmouth.'

'You may torture who you like,' William replied defiantly, 'but the document will be found in Portsmouth, to which it has already travelled under the protection of a man of my own. He has instructions to see that it falls into the hands of de Lucy, should we not reach Portsmouth within the week. Likewise if we arrive there in your custody. But if we are allowed to embark as planned, you have my word that the document will be launched overboard somewhere in mid-Channel, having first been torn into several pieces and thrown into the prevailing wind.'

'You were ever a tricky, slimy, ungrateful and treacherous pile of dirt!' de Beaumont yelled back.

William rose slightly in the saddle to give him a mock bow. 'I take that as a compliment, given its origin in the mouth of the man who taught me what underhand dealing really involves. Now, will you let us on our way, or do you wish to hang when King Henry learns that you allowed his queen to escape?'

Five days later, after a mercifully mild voyage along the north coast of Brittany and down into the Bay of Biscay, a rousing cheer went up from the passengers lining the port bulwarks as La Rochelle harbour came into sight. The morning sun bounced off the gilt armour of a large body of knights awaiting them on the quayside. As the deckhands leaped for the bollards and secured the hawsers, William took Eleanor's arm and helped her up onto the cobbles. From there they walked as steadily as five days on the ocean permitted towards the tall, grinning and sternly handsome young man on horseback who William had last seen as a teenager exchanging training blows with his son Hugh in the courtyard of Poitiers Palace.

Hugh was still mounted as Prince Richard slid from his courser's saddle and embraced his mother, giving thanks to God for her safe delivery.

'You must thank this man also,' Eleanor replied graciously as she gestured towards William.

Richard gave him a courtly bow. 'I believe that your son has reason to be proud of his ancestry. You may dismount and embrace your father, Hugh.'

Hugh did so, but before he could reach William he was intercepted by his mother Adele, who smothered him with a tight hug and shrieked her delight at being reunited with her first-born. Hugh's face turned bright red as he looked appealingly towards William. 'Please get her off me, Father. I do not cut a very knightly figure being coddled by my mother.'

XVII

The narrow streets of Canterbury were overflowing on that hot July morning. The king was on his way, but in a manner that had never before been witnessed. Humble tradespeople jostled with the wealthier sort to get a good view of what was about to occur. Pie sellers, pickpockets and prostitutes went about their business as they always did when crowds gathered, but today their marks had eyes only for what was about to pass. A king was about to submit to a flogging.

Just outside the town's West Gate, at the doors of St Dunstan's Parish Church, King Henry dismounted and handed his crown to his almoner. Then he entered the old town barefoot, clad only in simple hose, with just an undershirt to keep the hot sun from his back. The crowd buzzed and trilled with excitement as he came into sight, walking carelessly through the muddy puddles left by overnight rain, but taking great pains to skirt round the piles of horse manure and human detritus that lay beneath the overhanging eaves. There were murmurs of 'Assassin', 'Judas' and 'Shame!' from the less inhibited of the bystanders, but Henry ignored them as he walked on, bare-headed and humbled, through the narrow space that appeared before him as the crowd parted to allow him to progress to the great cathedral.

Entering by the west door, he dropped to his knees and crawled up the nave, packed to capacity with clerics, town officials and local worthies. When he reached the transept, he turned left and made his way, on all fours, into the Chapel of St Benedict, to the altar before which Thomas Becket had been hacked down. To either side of the altar stood bishops, monks and other clergy, fronted by Gilbert Foliot, Bishop of London, who was bearing a large rod cut from a local willow tree.

Henry was here, as promised some years since, to finally do penance for whatever part he had played in the death of a former friend and holy man who had been declared first a martyr, and then a saint. The monks from the adjoining priory had been keeping a tally, and over seven hundred miracles had already been recorded at this shrine for a fallen archbishop. The first had occurred within hours of his death, when a superstitious local man had dipped a cloth in Becket's blood and taken it home for his ailing wife, who had mixed it with water before drinking it. Her almost immediate recovery had encouraged a flood of pilgrims to the site, to kiss the stonework of Thomas's sepulchre in the hope of a cure or a blessing. The more gullible had bought phials of red liquid alleged to contain diluted spots of the healing fluid.

Thomas Becket was now revered throughout Europe, and his brutal death was being reviled as a sin against God. Henry was lucky not to have been excommunicated, and his nation placed under interdict; had the papacy not currently been experiencing a conflict between two rival claimants to the Holy See, then both punishments might already have been inflicted. Even Henry's daughter Eleanor, married to King Alfonso of Castile, had instructed that a mural be painted on the wall of her personal chapel of San Nicolas de Soria, depicting the martyrdom.

Henry looked up at Bishop Foliot and asked for a blessing for his sins, to which Foliot replied, 'What be they, my son?'

Henry bowed his head, then called out in a loud voice, 'I confess me of the sin of pride, that led to wild and wicked oaths concerning the blessed martyr who was my friend, and whose mortal remains lie here entombed. I do confess me that these words led certain others to mistake my true meaning, and out of an excess of devotion to my unworthy self they did travel to this holy place, and there commit the dreadful act that robbed the nation of the most blessed and holy man who ever graced it. For this I seek to do penance by the mortifying of my weak flesh, in the hope that Almighty God will have mercy on the immortal soul of this true penitent and preserve him from the fires of Hell. And so proceed.'

Bishop Foliot stepped forward, raised the rod, and brought it down gently five times onto Henry's back. Then he handed it to a minor bishop, who did the same, followed by the remaining bishops. Then it was the turn of the eighty monks of Canterbury, who were allowed three strokes each. By prior agreement the blows were symbolic only, since otherwise they would between them have committed regicide. Even so, the simple fabric of the humble shirt on Henry's back was in shreds as the clerics moved silently from the side chapel, leaving Henry alone.

Having deposited a bag of gold on the top of the tomb, Henry knelt back in supplication and spent the night reciting endless *pater nosters*, interspersed with prayers to God to grant him more humility in his dealings with others, and to stem the outbursts of wild temper that sometimes overcame him.

The hours passed sadly and silently until he felt a warm glow on his back, and saw a shaft of light falling on Becket's tomb. It was the first sunlight of the day creeping down the quire through the massive east window, and Henry sat back on his heels with a sigh of relief. Then he froze in terror when he heard a soft footfall behind him, and turned quickly in the expectation of being confronted by the angry wraith of the dead prelate. Instead it was a nervous page, sent to advise him that his horse was saddled and waiting outside, and that the mayor of Canterbury was offering him a breakfast worthy of someone who had spent all night in penance.

While consuming more cheese and hot bread than was good for him, Henry was told that the first miracle had already occurred, at almost the same time that he had been receiving his token lashes. King William of Scotland had been captured in battle, and was offering to hand back all his conquered lands and retreat behind his original borders in exchange for his freedom.

Henry cleared his mouth briefly and expressed his satisfaction. 'Let us hope that other miracles occur within the minds of my wicked and ungrateful sons,' he murmured, then set about carving more cheese from the block.

One wicked and ungrateful son had already demonstrated that he was a worthy branch of a brutal tree that had been planted by his distant ancestor Duke William of Normandy, although in Richard's case the victims dwelt in Aquitaine. The lengthy absence of their duchess had made them restive, and they had no reason to love the haughty and overbearing son who treated them like peasants, taxed them to the hilt in order to fund a permanent army whose foot soldiers were the last word in cruelty, and showed no sign of departing soon, in order that they might stage an uprising in his absence.

When Eleanor and her party finally reached Poitiers there was general rejoicing, but it was noticeable that everyone seemed relieved when Richard took his leave, accompanied as ever by Hugh, and returned to Aquitaine. It was some months later before some of her senior nobles took it upon themselves to warn her of Richard's famed brutality against those who opposed his will in Aquitaine, urging her not to allow him to return to Poitou in order to inflict the same on them.

Without giving reasons she announced to her immediate entourage that they would be travelling to Bordeaux without delay, since this was where she intended to establish her court. The handsome young man who eagerly met them in the courtyard as they dismounted and embraced his mother with loving endearments looked nothing like the merciless warrior that his reputation portrayed. He was as tall and slender as he had been upon their reunion in La Rochelle the previous year, and was still graced with light auburn hair that came with a well-tended beard, and blue eyes that twinkled. He detached himself from his mother's embrace and smiled warmly at William and Adele.

'You have raised a son of whom to be proud, and I thank you for allowing Hugh to follow me as my squire these past few years. One more battle and I will no doubt knight him.'

'One more battle and he may be dead,' William muttered.

Adele looked around. 'Where exactly *is* our son?' she asked nervously.

Richard laughed. 'He is awaiting us in the Great Hall, supervising the celebration dinner I have ordered in honour of your arrival. Being Hugh, he is no doubt sampling a few of the dishes in advance. And of course I remember the beautiful young lady by your side — little Joan.'

'Not quite so little, as you can see,' William replied, 'and the knight accompanying her, you may also recall, is Ralph de Coutances, who seeks her hand in marriage once he has proved himself worthy.'

'He is welcome here,' said Richard warmly, 'and should he care to join my armed company, he will not be lacking in opportunities to prove the strength of his sword arm.'

'I was advised, while in Poitiers, that there have been several serious uprisings here in Aquitaine,' Eleanor said diplomatically as they made their way through the great oak doors into the entrance hall.

Richard shrugged. 'A few, but when word got out that I was not in the habit of taking prisoners, they somehow seemed to falter. I hope that you did not have the misfortune to encounter any of their remains hanging from minor palace walls during the latter part of your journey?'

Eleanor shuddered and shook her head. 'Was it necessary to react with such brutality?'

Richard grinned. 'You enjoyed a peaceful passage once you crossed the border from Poitou, did you not? Either one rules with an iron fist, or not at all.'

'You remind me of your father,' she replied with a grudging smile, 'but do not regard that as a compliment.'

'How goes the miserable old bastard? Has he yet bedded my intended bride, are you aware?'

'Alys is said to still be in Devizes, no doubt wondering when she will be allowed to marry her royal prince,' Eleanor advised him with a worried frown. 'Since the Clifford whore died, Henry is rumoured to be dallying with de Balliol's daughter Annabel, but then there are so many rumours regarding his mistresses.'

'Including Alys of France,' Richard muttered. 'He surely can no longer pretend that she is intended as a bride for me. Not only has he kept her from me for several years, but he shames me in the eyes of Christendom. King Philip of France has sent several delegations here in recent months, demanding that I honour the terms of the treaty my father negotiated. He hints that she may no longer be a maid, thanks to my disgusting father. Were I to marry her now, there would no doubt be accusations of incest.'

'Can we not talk of more pleasant matters?' Eleanor grimaced as they mounted the stairs towards the Great Hall, from which a commanding voice could be heard ordering the servers about.

'The duchess shall of course have pride of place beside your master, but please leave two seats vacant alongside them, for my parents. My mother attends the Duchess Eleanor, and my father is her adviser. Do not place them as if they were mere servants, or it shall go ill with you. Now set about the trenchers, ere they arrive and find us wanting!'

'All *we* are wanting is to be reunited with our son!' William called out from the doorway.

Hugh turned with a broad smile and hurried down the hall to embrace them. The hugs and welcomes over, William stood back and admired what he saw.

'You have turned into the sort of man that my uncle hoped I would become,' he smiled at Hugh. 'The life of a warrior was not to my liking, but it was obvious even when you were a small boy that this would be the life you would follow. Fortunately for him, your younger brother Robert is destined to remain behind in England, to manage the estate when he is of suitable age. As for you, your master advises us that you may shortly be knighted.'

'When I am, may I use our estate name, or must I acquire another one? Only "Sir Hugh Repton" has a nice ring to it, does it not?'

William gave him a sympathetic frown. 'You were perhaps not to know, but the estate of Repton was taken from us by King Henry when I first took the side of Queen Eleanor. Your younger brother Robert has been allowed to remain on it by the new estate owners, who I believe are the Church. He will no doubt develop into a fine manager of both animals and crops, and a dedicated woodsman who has already proved himself able to supply a local abbey with timber in payment of the tithes due to it. But I no longer have any title left to bequeath to you.'

'You may soon be able to choose a more exotic title,' Richard reminded him as he waved the company into their allotted seats around the board. He signalled for the servers waiting in the doorway from the kitchen stairs to bring in the first round of salvers bearing dishes of salmon and langoustines.

'Your meaning?' Eleanor enquired as she dipped her fingers delicately into the bowl of lemon water in front of her.

'A Crusade!' Richard replied enthusiastically. 'The Pope is urging all Christian leaders to journey to Jerusalem, which is under threat. Young Hugh here may well be knighted as "Hugh of Jerusalem", or perhaps "Hugh of Antioch".'

'Either name would be an abomination,' Eleanor objected fiercely. 'I never saw Jerusalem, but I was for some time in Antioch, and my memories of it are of endless swarms of flies and heat that would fell an ox. I was much younger then, of course, but I would warn you most earnestly against proceeding beyond Byzantium.'

'It is rumoured that even my father has hopes of joining with Philip of France under the banner of Rome to rally to the Christian cause out there,' Richard argued, earning a derisive snort from his mother.

'Then let him do so, since he has been promising that ever since the death of Becket. It will hopefully be the death of him, and then *all* our combined estates can hope to have you as their new ruler.'

'You forget that I have three brothers to whom my father gives unjust preference.'

Eleanor reached out to place a hand on his sleeve. 'Your father was ever a fool, and a poor judge of men. No doubt he is even now seeking to bring Henry into line, while Geoffrey begs for the freedom to rule Brittany, and John fumbles with the latest serving wench to catch his eye — assuming that he returns alive from Ireland. *You* are the best suited to inherit from your father, Richard, so no more foolish talk of Crusades.'

Back in England Henry was feeling decidedly more confident, since his very public penance in Canterbury, than he had for some years. William of Scotland was back where he belonged, and there were no more uprisings being reported in Normandy. In a fit of generosity, Henry finally gave in to Geoffrey's pleas to be allowed to once again cross the Channel, ostensibly to take up his royal inheritance of Brittany. But several weeks later it was reported that Geoffrey had passed through the Vexin on his way south to Paris, and it was feared that he had joined his rebellious older brother, the Young Henry, in league with Philip Augustus of France.

Henry's temper was not improved when John returned from Ireland with his tail between his legs, blaming his lack of success on others, when in fact his arrogance and cruelty towards those Irish nobles who had formerly been friendly towards their English masters had been the true cause. But John knew how to play his father, and never missed an opportunity to assure him of his love and loyalty, compared with the scant regard given to him by his brothers, who were rumoured to be skulking in France and making plans to carve up Henry's painstakingly acquired empire among themselves. Rumours began to reach Paris that the 'baby' of the family, John, was receiving lavish gifts from their father, including strategic fortresses such as the castle of Nottingham, and was quietly boasting that he was now the favoured son, and would, upon their father's death, inherit England and Normandy at the very least.

In their bitterness Young Henry and Geoffrey also made much of the fact that while John had become their father's favourite, there was little doubt that their mother had a soft spot for Richard, who was the only one of the royal sons enfeoffed of any of the estates that their father had originally prized so highly. Philip Augustus of France clearly had much to gain strategically by stirring up the heir apparent Henry and the treacherous and resentful Geoffrey, and he finally talked them into a joint attack on Aquitaine and Poitiers from the east.

The combined assault came as a complete surprise to Richard and Eleanor. They were obliged to respond hastily to the fall of the border fortress of Ségur, which gave access to either Poitou or Aquitaine, depending upon whether one headed further west or turned south. Richard opted to strengthen the defensive walls of Bordeaux, behind which he installed Eleanor and her retinue. He then rode north with an increasingly large army that snowballed into a massive force as it collected both volunteers and conscripts.

News of his approaching horde was enough to divert his enemies' attention from the almost defenceless Poitou, and they turned south to do battle. The ensuing clash of arms lasted less than two hours, but it was three hours after that before Richard's men had finished dispatching the last of the wounded, and hanging their prisoners from every wall, post and doorway they could find. Two days later, Richard and Hugh clattered back into Bordeaux at the head of a victorious army. They leapt off their mounts in the stable yard, turning to embrace their loved ones, and discovering that men covered in the blood of their fallen foes were not particularly attractive.

'Dear God in Heaven,' Adele muttered as she swallowed a throat full of bile, 'I hope that none of that blood on Hugh is his own!'

'Behold the newly knighted "Hugh of Limoges"!' Richard called out. 'He fought bravely, and killed at least half a dozen that I saw for myself. There were undoubtedly more than that, but I was somewhat distracted in killing those who came for me. But Aquitaine and Poitou are safe from any French bastard or their traitorous allies!'

'Are you proud of me, Father?' Hugh preened.

William hung his head. 'I am pleased that you have achieved your ambition, but I fear for your future.'

'And I must lose no time in getting back to Poitou,' Eleanor muttered out of earshot of Richard, 'in case they fear that Richard will seek revenge on those nobles who sided with Geoffrey.'

There was another favourable outcome for Richard from the unsuccessful campaign against him in Limousin. On his return journey towards Paris, the Young Henry was stricken with a violent stomach ailment that nothing seemed to remedy. He was taken by litter to an abbey close to Limoges, and although he was still only in his late twenties even he, along with his household, realised that the end was close. He made confession and received the last rites, then in a somewhat melodramatic gesture of penitence for the years in which he had opposed his father, he prostrated himself naked on the floor before a crucifix. Although he asked to see his father one final time, to beg his forgiveness, King Henry suspected a trap and refused to cross the Channel. Young Henry died clasping a ring his father had sent instead as a sign of his forgiveness.

When informed that his almost lifelong favourite son had passed away, Henry came as close as anyone could remember to dissolving in grief, and was heard to murmur, 'He cost me much, but I wish he had lived to cost me more.'

Richard's response, when advised of Henry's death, was a simple nod and a callous observation. 'This leaves just two more — when Geoffrey and John have been overcome, my father will have no choice but to die a miserable old man who knows that his wife's favourite has finally won the game.'

XVIII

'I should perhaps be commiserating with you on the loss of a brother,' King Philip Augustus remarked with a sardonic smile as Richard was admitted. The prince strolled confidently down the blue carpet inside the Audience Chamber of the Palais de la Cité before bowing. He raised his head with a triumphant smirk, then took the gestured seat.

'Henry was never a brother to me, Philip. Perhaps more to you, since you were behind his recent unsuccessful foray against my lands in Aquitaine and Poitou. Indeed, I believe I espied some fleur-de-lis banners among those trodden into the mud following my victory.'

'Are you here to gloat, or perhaps seek ransom money for those taken prisoner?'

'I took no prisoners, as you will have heard. If you wish to send men to rob your own dead, you need now only follow the stench from their rotting remains.'

'Ever the poet. So what brings you here?'

'I am here to offer to pay homage to you in return for Aquitaine, Normandy and Anjou.'

Philip turned slightly in his throne seat to give Richard a hard stare. 'Aquitaine is already yours — even your father would concede that. But Normandy and Anjou were your brother Henry's, were they not? I was not aware that King Henry has named a new heir to them yet. And you forget the continued presence here in Paris of your other brother, Geoffrey.'

'I do not forget Geoffrey — I merely despise him as a weakling and an indifferent ruler of Brittany, which I plan to overrun in due course.'

'Such ambition! And what of the other brother — John?'

'What of him? He could not even put down a rebellion in the bogs of Ireland, so he is of no account.'

'Rumour has reached me that your father intends to make him his heir, since he is now the favourite son. I also hear rumours regarding my sister Alys, who you have yet to marry.'

Richard finally lost what little diplomacy and even temper he had summoned up for the occasion, and thumped the arm of his chair angrily. 'We will progress with this conversation more fruitfully if we cease wasting each other's time, Philip. I want my father's lands, and I am prepared to do homage to you for them once you have helped me to take them by force.'

Philip fell silent, then his face softened. 'I was not speaking lightly regarding the matter of my sister. My family is shamed by what your father is alleged to have reduced her to, and you have done nothing to guard either her virtue or her reputation throughout Christendom.'

'As to what my father is alleged to have done, that is a matter for his conscience. You should seek redress from him — as indeed you will be doing if you assist me in bringing him down.'

'And once Alys is released into your custody — whether she be soiled goods or no — you will marry her?'

'If that will secure your alliance in my overall plans, then of course.'

'If I were to send word to your father that either Alys be returned here intact within two months, or her dowry of Berry reverts to France, what would be your reaction?'

'I would happily take both Alys *and* Berry, but I doubt that King Henry will part with her. I have long since regretted my descent from his lusty loins.'

'But you have also long revered your mother, Eleanor. What says she of your journey here?'

'She may not even be aware of it. I certainly did not require her permission to leave Poitiers, from where I departed on my journey to Paris.'

There was another lengthy silence, at the end of which Philip smiled at some inner thought before announcing his conclusion. 'We shall let your father set the agenda, Richard. Either Alys is returned, and you and she are married, or she is not, in which case France will be at war with England.'

'And if she is returned and we are *not* married?' Richard asked hesitantly.

Philip's face darkened. 'Then you will not have my support. Indeed, you may not even retain your freedom. Bear that in mind before you play me false.'

Eleanor's laughter was hollow, somewhat strained and nervous. But she was determined to put a brave face on the situation that had arisen, if only to lift the spirits of those around her.

'Since Richard chose to take himself off without advising me of his intentions, we can only surmise what his reaction would have been. Since rumour has it that he is in Paris with King Philip, we can perhaps conjecture that he is seeking his assistance to attack his father's estates in England and Normandy. He would not take it well were I to claim suzerainty over Aquitaine — going behind his back, as it were — and we have all borne witness to the savagery of which he is capable when angered. I think that our position is clear, and we must decline — not that I am anxious to be seen to do my husband's bidding anyway.'

A despatch had recently come from Henry in England, demanding that Eleanor take over the governance of Aquitaine, of which she was the notional duchess anyway. Henry wanted her to hold it in the name of her youngest son, John, to whom he intended to bequeath it. Everyone was fearful of the likely reaction to this of the merciless Richard, even though Eleanor was his mother and Richard was generally regarded as her favourite son — indeed the only son to whom she now had regular access. Young Henry was dead, John was following his father like a faithful lapdog, and Geoffrey was still in Paris, where he might, for all they knew, have joined forces with Richard. It would hardly be good for their immediate futures to seek to deprive Richard of his notional title to Aquitaine. The title was one thing, but actual military supremacy was another.

William and Adele had another perspective, however, and William chose his words carefully.

'With respect, my lady, we must also consider King Henry's likely response were you to refuse his command. You are currently safe back behind the walls of Poitiers here, and thanks to Richard and his men you may expect any attempt on your husband's part to seize your person to be met with a most brutal resistance. For that reason you are safe here, and you would be ill advised to thwart whatever plans Richard may have. So Henry can only respond to any refusal on your part with impotent rage. But some of us still have a continuing vulnerability to that rage.'

Adele choked back a tear and nodded. 'For all we know, your husband has already sought out our younger son Robert and had him imprisoned — or worse. He dispossessed us of our estate at Repton, and sold it to the Church. We have no knowledge of what fate may have befallen our youngest.'

'I may be able to reassure you there,' Ralph de Coutances advised the company from where he sat beside Joan. 'As you may know, Repton falls within the See of Lincoln, of which until recently my brother Walter was the bishop. He is now transferred to Rouen, and the See currently lies vacant through Henry's neglect. But that neglect works to our advantage, since the estates held by the See remain undisturbed. The latest news I had from my brother was that Repton thrives under good management, and makes regular and substantial returns to its overlord the bishop, by way of timber carried annually to the Priory of Lenton, half a day's ride away. My brother is blessed with regular correspondence from the priests who he appointed in his time, and who remain loyal and affectionate towards him. At my request he maintains contact with the abbot of Lenton Priory, and the reports are all favourable, in the sense that Henry has made no move against your son Robert, who is said to show promise as a skilled and devoted estate manager.'

'Thank you for that,' William replied warmly, 'and we are indeed fortunate to have such regular reports. But that does not prevent Henry taking his revenge, should we not comply with his request.'

'With all due regard to yourself, William,' Eleanor replied, 'the request was made of *me*. While you are very important to us here in Poitiers, it is to be doubted that Henry has you in the forefront of his mind when he is seeking to come to terms with a rebellion by his most warlike of sons and the King of France.'

'That puts me in my place,' William replied sheepishly, 'but do you still value my advice?'

'Of course, as I have ever done,' Eleanor reassured him. 'So how should I reply to Henry's demand?'

'With silence,' William advised her. 'This will unsettle him more than anything, and you are well protected here, in the south-west of France, and with Richard barely a week's ride away. Henry could hardly have expected you to agree, and your silence will simply underline the strength of your ongoing relationship with Richard. As for Geoffrey, he would seem to have taken himself off the battlefield for the time being, and was last heard of playing the gallant English knight in Paris.'

Two months later came the momentous news that Geoffrey had entered into one list too many, and had died during the grand melee of a tourney held in the grounds of the Palais de la Cité. There were now only two royal sons left to contest the inheritance, and a vacancy for a ruler over Brittany. However, Geoffrey's widow Constance was in residence in the ducal palace in Nantes, and was expected to deliver her third child to Geoffrey in the weeks to come. The first two had been girls, but the birth of a boy would create an obvious successor to Geoffrey, unless either Richard or Henry overran the duchy and claimed it for themselves.

The household in Poitiers waited anxiously for news of the latest outbreak of violence somewhere in a bordering duchy or dukedom. It therefore came as a considerable relief when Eleanor was advised that her attendance, representing Aquitaine, was required at a peace conference to be conducted under the auspices of Pope Clement III, at a place that was yet to be determined.

This new initiative was not the result of any desire on the part of his Holiness to reunite a dysfunctional family; rather it had to do with recent events in the Holy Land. The new Saracen warrior Saladin had finally captured Jerusalem, and the Pope had proclaimed a Third Crusade to retake this icon of the

Christian faith. Many of the leading knights of Europe had been persuaded, or shamed, into taking the Cross, and they included Philip and Richard.

The English prince in particular showed great enthusiasm for the challenge, and was anxious to restore English honour in the eyes of Rome, given that his father had vowed to embark on a Crusade as one of his penances for the murder of Becket, but had never got around to honouring that vow. But the Pope was fearful that Richard would not feel easy about departing for what could be a two-year campaign in the Middle East, leaving his father free to pillage and repossess Aquitaine and Poitiers while promoting the interests of his declared heir John in England and Normandy. Pope Clement therefore set himself up as the family peacemaker, and La Ferté-Bernard, a township to the north-east of Le Mans, was designated as the meeting place.

Although modest in size, the township possessed both a castle and a chateau. The Pope chose the latter as his conference venue, given the relative luxury of the accommodation that it could provide while he made it his base. This left the rival factions to argue from a distance regarding who was to occupy the castle, but eventually — with much misgiving — both Henry, accompanied as ever by John, and Richard in the company of Philip of France, agreed to occupy a wing each of the spacious fortress. The nearby Cistercian abbey willingly opened its doors to Eleanor and her party, and it was from there, early on the first morning set aside for negotiations, that she set off nervously in company with William, Adele, Ralph de Coutances and several men at arms to ensure their personal safety.

Eleanor was shocked to the core by her first sight of the husband she had not laid eyes on for some twelve years. He was still overweight, but his customary ruddy complexion had been replaced by a grey pallor, and his once golden-brown hair hung limply from his skull to lie on the shoulders of his tunic as if grateful to have found a resting place. His hand appeared to tremble slightly as he raised a wine cup to his lips. John assured Eleanor that it contained a potion prescribed by a court physician at Caen to combat the stomach pains by which Henry was increasingly wracked.

It had been John who had first noticed his mother's entrance into the chamber designated for the meeting. He had sidled over with a smile that would have looked more in place on a fox as he embraced her perfunctorily and enquired after her health.

Eleanor smiled with a warmth that she did not feel, and assured him that she was in the peak of good health. 'Which is more than can be said for your father. What in God's name ails him?'

'It is a malady of the stomach, Mother. It gives him great agony, whenever he eats and whenever he is hungry. In short, the whole time; he is only half the man he used to be.'

Eleanor snorted. 'He was only ever half a man to begin with, and his stomach was ever in peril of what he stuffed into it. Has his temper improved?'

'Not when he is in one of his gripes,' John replied.

Henry seemed to become aware of the group seated to the rear of the chamber, and called out, 'Leave your faithless mother be, and get over here — I need more of this potion if I am to see out the morning!'

John scuttled away, but was only halfway towards where Henry sat, doubled over in pain, when there was a movement from the side door. Richard stalked in, head held high and with a supercilious smirk on his face. 'Out of my way, baby brother!'

he sneered at John as he hurriedly completed his retreat to his father's corner. Richard paused briefly. 'Good morning, Father — *so* nice to see you and Mother in the same room again!' He then stalked purposefully across to Eleanor and held her in a warm embrace as he whispered, 'I trust that Aquitaine is in all ways ready to celebrate my triumphal return?'

'Where is Philip of France?' Eleanor asked.

Richard grinned. 'You will see him soon enough.'

As if to prove him correct, a herald decked from head to foot in the blue and gold of France, with fleur-de-lis emblems emblazoned on his tunic, called out, 'Pray silence for the entry of his most gracious Philip Augustus, Sovereign of France!' He then stepped lithely to one side as Philip entered, dressed in all his royal finery and with a look of mild disdain on his face, as if examining a blocked privy.

Only then did the Pope's legate put in an appearance. 'His Holiness has instructed me to conduct this first meeting, in the hope that broad grounds can be identified for a more detailed peace treaty to be concluded under the auspices of his holy office,' he explained to the assembled company.

However, it rapidly became apparent that his Holiness was not likely to be unduly troubled. No sooner had the legate announced the opening of the proceedings, when Philip of France bellowed across the room at Henry, 'Where is my sister, and what have you done with her?'

'She was intended as a bride for me, you libidinous old goat!' Richard screamed in support.

Eleanor cackled. 'Your sons know you too well, Henry!'

'At least I didn't lie with my own uncle!' Henry responded.

'Please, let us not descend into mere abuse!' the legate pleaded.

'My sister has been cruelly abused by this old fool who cannot even control his own sons!' shouted Philip. 'Thanks to him and his disgusting tastes, Europe has been reduced to a battlefield that knows no limits. Before we even begin to agree peace terms, I want my sister returned to me in the same maidenly state that she was in when she left Paris.'

'Assuming that *your* father didn't have her first!' Henry yelled back.

This was all the provocation that Philip needed to draw his sword, followed by the four men at arms who attended him. Henry's attendants formed a defensive ring around him, and John drew a sword as he called upon his attendants to prepare to engage the French.

The legate raised a crozier in the air and called out at the top of his lungs, 'God's curse and eternal damnation in the fires of Hell to whoever draws first blood!'

This was sufficient to cause everyone who had unsheathed a weapon to return it to its rightful place, as angry and defiant glares crossed the chamber like silent arrows.

Eleanor turned to Adele and whispered, 'Time for us to withdraw, I suggest.'

XIX

Back at their abbey, Eleanor called for wine and drank her first draught with a hand that was still shaking. 'There is as much chance of a lasting peace agreement being reached as there is of me flying across this chamber,' she declared. 'We should lose no time in returning to Poitiers and seeing to its defences.'

They waited in fearful anticipation for an army that never came — not Philip's, not Henry's and not even Richard's. Finally, in the mid-morning light of the sixth day, a small group of horsemen clattered into the courtyard, led by Richard. Eleanor was seated by a window, and called to the others as she looked down.

'Here comes "the prodigal son", as Henry once called him. In truth, he was the only one who ever showed him due respect, and the only one fit to inherit. Let us see what shambles remains of what used to be the Plantagenet empire.'

They waited longer than would have been necessary for Richard to reach the main hall on the first floor had he proceeded at his usual pace, taking two stairs at a time. They were looking at each other nervously when the double doors opened, and a page appeared, looking uncomfortable. After a moment's hesitation, he called out, 'Please make welcome the King of England, Duke of Normandy and Aquitaine, and Count of Poitou.'

A grinning Richard strode through the doorway.

It was Eleanor who gave voice to the obvious question. 'May we assume that your father is dead, or has there been some miraculous change of favour on his part?'

'Both,' Richard smirked as he walked to the side table and helped himself to a mug of wine.

'Did you kill him?' his mother demanded, horrified.

He shook his head. 'His stomach finally did, but not before we had become reconciled and he'd declared me to be his heir. In front of holy witnesses, what's more. Mind you, given that the only alternative was John, and that he'd fled the battlefield several hours previously, Father *was* rather limited in his choice.'

'You mentioned a battlefield,' William intervened. 'Did you defeat your father in battle?'

'I never got the chance, although we did mop up some of his stray men at arms just this side of Alencon. But Father made a run for it — or rather his litter did, since he was too weak to ride a horse, apparently — and for some reason he made south towards Anjou. I think he knew he was dying, and he wanted to do so where he was born. He got as far as Chinon, where they had to unload him so he could receive the last rites.'

'Were you present at his deathbed?' Eleanor asked in a voice wavering with emotion.

Richard nodded. 'Not just me, but also Philip of France and a whole gaggle of clergymen and physicians. Father was quite the most generous and co-operative that I've ever seen him, but then he *was* about to enter Purgatory for all his sins.'

Despite herself Eleanor choked on a sob. Adele draped a comforting arm across her shoulders, while glaring angrily at Richard for his lack of tact. William took advantage of the silence and urged Richard to tell the rest of his story.

'Nothing *to* tell, really. Father asked for my forgiveness, so I thought it best to ask him for mine in exchange. Then Philip started going on about that dreadful Alys again. Father promised that he would give orders for her to be handed over to a suitable guardian, to await my return from the Crusade in order that we may then be married. Then he declared to the world that I was heir to all his kingdoms, duchies and so on, and we did the kiss of peace thing over a holy relic that someone seemed to have available. So here I am.'

'You mentioned the Crusade,' William began. 'Are you still minded to honour the vow you took?'

Richard smiled and nodded. 'In company with my good friend and ally Philip Augustus of France. It's perhaps the best way to ensure that neither of us takes unfair advantage of the absence of the other from his kingdoms. But I will need to raid the Treasury first, in order to confirm that I have the means to fund an army. It would not be good for my first task as King of England and Duke of Normandy to be the imposition of a tax on the people.' He turned to William. 'On that subject, are you aware of who is currently the Chancellor of England? I've been here in Poitou and Aquitaine for so long that I've lost touch with matters over there.'

'I left England myself shortly after Becket's death,' William reminded him, 'so I'm not able to advise you on that, I'm afraid.'

'No matter,' Richard replied breezily. 'I shall simply appoint my own man and order him to empty the Treasury into my saddlebags. Likewise the justiciar's office — that must be worth a good few pounds from the highest bidder.'

'You intend to sell off the highest offices in England?' Eleanor enquired disbelievingly.

Richard poured himself more wine. 'Not just in England — here in Poitou, and also in my other possessions. I shall need all the money I can raise in order to equip an army to outshine that of Philip of France.'

'And in order to win back Jerusalem?' William prompted him.

'That also,' Richard conceded. 'But at this very moment I have need to rest. It has been a very tiring few days, but I suppose it's been worth it. It's not every day that you finally come into the inheritance that's been denied you for years.'

With that he swept from the chamber, and only then did William realise that for once he was not followed several feet behind by his eldest son. With rising alarm he turned to Ralph de Coutances, who had originally entered the chamber a moment or two after Richard. 'My son Hugh — has he returned safely? Only he was not with Richard, as he usually is.'

'Have no fear — he returned with us, and was carrying a considerable amount of booty in the form of swords, shields and other pieces of armoury that Henry's soldiers abandoned in their haste to escape us at Alencon,' Ralph assured him. 'I last saw him in the stables, demanding that his trophies be locked away for safekeeping. And now, if you would excuse me? I hope that your daughter eagerly awaits my return, although she does not appear to be in the present company.'

'She may be found in the chapel, praying for your safe delivery,' Adele told him. 'When we were leaving that dreadful place where the Pope hoped to hold his peace conference, we saw you in Richard's company, milling around and planning to chase the English army that Henry had brought with him. As usual she was apprehensive that you might be killed, so she took herself off to spend her time in prayer until your safe return. I think we may conclude from her actions that you and she will make a contented match in marriage.'

'Once William gives his consent,' Ralph replied.

William smiled. 'Once I know where I shall be destined to take the rest of my family, we may discuss the issue further. Now, go and find Joan and reassure her of your continued life.'

Ralph walked hastily from the room with a broad smile of anticipation, and Adele turned to Eleanor. 'Will you return to England with King Richard, my lady? And will you still require a lady to attend you now that you are the queen dowager?'

Eleanor's face clouded over for a moment before she replied with carefully chosen words. 'I suspect that Richard has inherited some of his father's rashness along with his lands, and that I may continue to be of service to him in the matter of giving him sage advice, whether he feels that he needs it or not. So the answer to your question is "yes", dear Adele. I only hope that you wish to continue in my service now that I am an elderly widow approaching seventy years of age.'

'With all my heart, my lady,' Adele gushed. 'But will you still require William's wise lawyer's counsel?'

'No, but I have no doubt that Richard would benefit from it,' Eleanor replied. 'Leave that to me, since my impetuous son will be obliged to heed his mother's advice ere we leave Poitiers for England. He needs to have men who can be trusted around him.'

'Thank you, Your Majesty,' said William with a slight bow.

Eleanor beamed. 'You have not called me that for some years now, William, and there is certainly no need for it while we are conversing privily like this. But I must now prepare to be a queen once again, albeit in a different form — then of course I shall expect the customary form of address.'

Two days later, the castle rumour mill was thrown into fervent action when word reached every department of it that Prince John had arrived, accompanied by only two men at arms, and with a face more resembling that of an errant school pupil than the twenty-three-year-old brother of the new monarch. He and Richard spent several hours in private conversation, at the end of which William, Adele, Ralph de Coutances and Joan were among those summoned to the Great Hall for a set of proclamations.

Eleanor was seated between John and Richard, as if required, as their mother, to sort out some childish squabble between them. William was struck by how the lines of age seemed to have left her face as the two brothers appeared to have finally agreed to do as their mother told them. A herald called for silence.

Richard waved his arm regally in John's direction and announced, 'I am delighted to advise you all that the future of the kingdoms established by my late father is assured. The youngest two sons of that mighty monarch are united in an accord that will ensure perpetual peace for all our subjects.'

'I'll believe that when the Thames freezes over, and angels walk across it from Westminster to Southwark,' William whispered hoarsely in Adele's ear. She gestured for him to remain silent as Richard continued.

'My brother John is hereby appointed Count of Mortain, which he will rule under my suzerainty as part of my Duchy of Normandy. In England he is to retain those estates in which he was formally enfeoffed by our father, namely those in Cornwall, Derby, Devon, Dorset, Nottingham and Somerset, although he has agreed that during my absence on Crusade he will allow England to be supervised by our gracious mother, who shall be known as "Eleanor, Queen Dowager of England." Until my hoped-for safe return from the reconquest of Jerusalem, John shall be based in Mortain, from which he will keep a watchful eye on Normandy.

'My brother has also agreed to take in marriage the hand of Isabella, the Countess of Gloucester, whose grandfather was Count Robert of Gloucester. As those of you who are old enough will recall, he was the right-hand man of my own grandmother Matilda. This makes them both great-grandchildren of the first King Henry, and it was our father's wish that the family ties between our two great houses be strengthened by such an alliance. They were first betrothed at his insistence some three years ago, and when we travel back to England they shall be finally joined in marriage, prior to John returning to Mortain.

'There remains the matter of the succession, should I die on Crusade, and I can only make such provision as current circumstances permit. Our older brother Henry left no issue on his untimely death, and John of course remains currently unmarried, and therefore without lawful issue. But our brother Geoffrey, on his tragic demise during a tournament, left a widow who was then with child. That child proved to be a boy named Arthur, who I confirm as Duke of Brittany under the regency of his mother Constance, and the heir to all my territories.'

John's face was a picture of sullen compliance as Richard brought the proceedings to a close.

'That is all I have to announce at this time. You are all cordially invited to drink to the future of all our possessions, and to give thanks to God for this happy occasion. I shall be speaking privily with some of you on a later date, but for now that is all. The servers have placed wine at your disposal to the side of the hall, so please join with us in celebration.'

The following morning, William was not surprised to be summoned to Richard's private chambers. He was invited to take a seat and was handed a mug of wine by an attendant. Richard smiled, and William was reminded of a fox that Hugh had once proudly shot with an arrow as it stalked around the chicken run on their former estate.

'First of all, my grateful thanks for all you have done in my mother's service,' Richard said.

'And for your father before that,' William added.

'Precisely,' Richard concurred, 'and it is in connection with your service to my late father that I wish your advice and compliance.'

William knew better than to interrupt.

'To the best of my knowledge, the legal affairs of England are in utter turmoil,' he announced. 'The Chancery is allegedly headed by my bastard half-brother Geoffrey, and I doubt that he can even count, given the shambles reported to me regarding the state of the account rolls. I have been offered a considerable sum of money for the post by one of those who hang around me in hope of advancement. I have in mind appointing him as chancellor, since he can do no worse than his predecessor. There will in any case be nothing left in the Treasury once I get back over there for long enough to add its contents to my war chest. His name is William de Longchamp, and I may also seek further payment from him for the purely decorative title of "justiciar", since two others — Hugh de Puiset and William de Mandeville — have already paid their way into the same title. The third position will be purely for boasting purposes.'

'Do any of these men have the remotest experience in the administration of the justice system that your father strove so hard to implement, under my guidance?' William asked. His heart fell to his boots in contemplation of a court regime presided over by ignorant fops who had paid for the privilege.

'I doubt it,' Richard answered without any obvious sense of shame, 'which is why I require your services.'

'As a *fourth* justiciar?' William enquired, mortified.

Richard shook his head. 'No — as Chief Justice of England. The most senior of those who travel the country dealing with serious crime, and to whom all the other justices will be subservient. I have created the post with you in mind, since I have no faith in those who have paid for their titles.'

William almost demanded to know why, therefore, he had sold them their titular positions in the first place, but held his tongue. However, his face must have reflected his unease at what Richard was proposing, because the new king smiled reassuringly.

'I will not require any payment in return for your appointment,' he said.

'That is perhaps as well,' William grimaced, 'because I have no estate since your father confiscated Repton and handed it to the Church.'

'Ah, yes, the manor of Repton,' Richard continued. 'Ralph de Coutances tells me that it has been well managed by one of your sons while it has been under the suzerainty of the Bishop of Lincoln. I am well disposed to grant it back to you, along with your earldom, in return for your consent to the marriage of your daughter to Ralph de Coutances. Not that he requires it, of course, since Joan is well of age. But he needed mine, and was more than happy to make a generous donation towards my Crusade preparations.'

William hastily swallowed an angry outburst as he learned of what sounded like the sordid sale of his only daughter. He kept his face sternly expressionless as he advised Richard that he had been on the point of granting his consent anyway, and enquired further as to his proposed new duties.

'You will be largely free to decide on those for yourself, since no-one has previously occupied the position, so no precedent has been set. But I shall expect to receive assurances from others that serious crime has ceased to disgrace the image of England among civilised nations, and how you bring about that minor miracle will be a matter for you. But,' he added as he lowered his voice conspiratorially, 'my principal requirement is that you keep a wary eye on those who may be working in my brother's interests. I do not trust John not to make a bid for my crown while I am away in the Holy Land, and I am far from confident that he will remain in Mortain once my back is turned. You will of course have the power to bring about the conviction and execution of anyone in his pay who commits violence in order to enforce any attempted rule on his part. You may also rely on the support of my mother, acting as my Regent, at the head of a Regency Council that will contain the Justiciar de Longchamp and the Archbishop of Rouen, Walter de Coutances. He is of course the brother of your future son-in-law Ralph, and he was formerly Bishop of Lincoln. Do you accept on those terms?'

'I will need to discuss them with my wife,' William insisted, earning himself a knowing smirk from Richard.

'That should not occupy you for long, since my mother took the opportunity to explain what I had in mind to her a few moments before you arrived here. I am advised that the Countess of Repton is more than happy with what I propose.'

'You would seem to have more influence over my family than I do,' William muttered, far from content with the turn of events. 'May I also assume that you will be taking Hugh with you on Crusade?'

'You may. And bear in mind that by this means he might rise to great prominence, not to mention considerable wealth, and great estimation in the eyes of the Pope.'

'I will settle for him being returned alive,' William replied through gritted teeth.

Richard's face froze in what looked like irritation. 'I am relying on your stubbornness, and your refusal to be cowed, in your support for my cause, but do not seek to employ them against me. You are dismissed.'

William had fully reconciled himself to the changing circumstances by the time he became part of the mighty cavalcade that rode sedately out of Poitiers Palace on the first stage of its lengthy journey back to England. At its head were four lines of men at arms, three abreast and resplendent in the golden lion blazons of England. Behind them were three royal heralds who invited those who gathered in curiosity at crossroads and in village squares to make way for King Richard of England.

Behind the heralds were the honoured nobles who rode ahead of His Majesty himself. William was one of these, riding next to his recently acquired son-in-law Ralph de Coutances, whose bride Joan was several hundred yards behind them. She was riding among the court ladies immediately behind the litter bearing the lady who would in future sign her papers as 'Eleanor, by the grace of God, Queen of England'. Alongside the litter, riding as ever on the faithful palfrey that would be put out to gentle grazing retirement on their recently retrieved Derbyshire estate, was Adele, Countess of Repton, smiling at everyone they passed as she reminded herself that they were finally heading home.

The same thoughts were passing through William's head, but with a heavy flavouring of uncertainty and apprehension. He had his only daughter safely married off, and once they crossed the Channel she would take her rightful place as the lady of an extensive estate in Cornwall. But the sons were another concern altogether.

Riding somewhere behind him, in the glittering throng that surrounded the new King Richard on his way to his coronation, were a group of eager knights suitably attired in English surcoats. Their coursers proudly tossed their heads as they carried on their backs the cream of the royal house guards, whose pennants fluttered in the early morning breeze, and whose chainmail creaked in their saddles. In their centre was King Richard himself, proudly wearing the white surcoat with the red cross that depicted him as a Crusader knight.

One of that inner elite was William's own firstborn, Hugh, whose only ambition seemed to be to die valiantly and have stories written about him. William trembled as he tore his thoughts away from what horrible death might await him.

Then there was his other son, Robert, who would now be approaching early manhood, believing himself to be the son of the Steward of Repton, and totally ignorant of his true birthright as the second-born son of the lord of the manor. Adele would not stop chattering eagerly about being reunited with him, but William feared she would be disappointed when Robert struggled to free himself from the clutches of a seeming madwoman who claimed to be his mother.

But most of all William feared for England. After the many years during which two cousins, Matilda and Stephen, had reduced it to a wasteland in the struggle for the crown, it had endured the thirty-five-year reign of a despot who could not even engender affection in the hearts of his family. The nation was in desperate need of a strong but benevolent monarch who put the interests of his subjects first. Instead, they were destined to be ruled by a dreamer, a self-deluding romantic warrior who believed that he was commissioned by God to rescue Jerusalem for Christianity, and was prepared to stoop to any depths in order to finance his obsession. He had already begun to sell the highest offices in the realm to those with wealth without wisdom, money without morals, and no doubt there would be many such shameful transactions to follow once they reached Westminster. Richard was reported to have boasted that he would even sell London if he could find a buyer.

William had no option but to allow himself to be carried along by this new tide, as he had been by the old one. He was still alive, and he still possessed an estate. He had a wife to whom he was devoted, and he had three children, albeit two of them with uncertain futures.

In this rapidly degenerating world, perhaps this was all he could reasonably expect, but the next few years promised to be tumultuous. With that thought, he lifted his head and watched England grow closer with each horse-borne step.

A NOTE TO THE READER

Dear Reader,

Thank you for taking the time to read this fourth novel in a series of seven that between them cover the twelfth century, a period during which England was transformed beyond recognition. I hope that it lived up to your expectations. Once again the basic plot line was written for me by the events that really happened during one of the most unsettled periods of that tumultuous age.

As the so-called 'Anarchy' came to an end, and Henry Plantagenet blustered his way onto the throne, England was on its knees. It had endured famine, pestilence and endless warfare in which rival armies trampled down what few crops had survived a series of disastrous harvests. It welcomed the new monarch as 'Henricus Secundus', in the fervent hope that his accession meant a change of fortune for the nation. They were about to be bitterly disappointed.

Thanks to Hollywood, we have an image of Henry II as a dashing, romantic, argumentative, dynamic and charismatic man who charmed a beautiful woman into marriage, and was then cruelly betrayed by both her and their sons. He was portrayed in two major movies of the 1960s, both of which starred Peter O'Toole as Henry. In the first, *Becket*, O'Toole delivered a masterclass in overacting that earned, from one film critic, the observation that 'O'Toole played the king as though in mortal fear that someone was about to play the Ace'. Playing alongside him, as Becket, was Richard Burton, whose deadpan, emotionless portrayal of the Archbishop of Canterbury was equally false. Worst of all was the suggestion that Becket had, in his younger days, been a roistering companion of King Henry.

The real Henry Plantagenet was stocky, barrel-chested, foul-tempered, promiscuous and gluttonous. Hardly the romantic hero, but something about him attracted the young and very recently divorced Eleanor, Duchess of Aquitaine and Countess of Poitou. It may have been his libidinous reputation, since she was reputed to be similarly inclined, and had spent too long deprived of sexual fulfilment in the marriage bed of the ascetic King Louis of France. Their union promised much, and delivered little except eight children, seven of whom survived. Of these, four were boys who were mismanaged to the point of open rebellion.

In O'Toole's second sally at being Henry II, in *The Lion in Winter*, we see him as a middle-aged man in bitter conflict with his wife of many years, who is siding with their sons in the wreckage of their family life, while being held under house arrest by her own husband. This at least came closer to historical accuracy, although it is uncertain whether Eleanor was ever as gracious and regal as Katharine Hepburn portrayed her. The marriage of Henry and Eleanor had been a classic case of an irresistible force meeting an immoveable object, and it was not pretty. However, historians make much of the undoubted fact that under Henry's rule, our 'common law' legal system experienced its birth pains, given Henry's determination to enforce his will on the unruly and troublesome barons who hung around his court, and were never to be entirely trusted. It was during the thirty-five years of his reign that England acquired the 'assize' system under which royal justices toured the country implementing the same laws in all corners of the land, acting as personal representatives of the 'King in Curia'. Other aspects of the 'accusatorial' system of criminal justice which we now take for granted (e.g. jury trial and the presumption of innocence) would follow during the reign of Henry's youngest son, John. His reign is the subject of the sixth novel in this series, *The Road to Runnymede*, but the seeds were first sown by Henry II.

This was almost certainly his only real legacy to the nation that he ruled with such ill grace, betrayed by his own blindness regarding what was going on in his own domestic surroundings. Like Charlemagne in a previous age, he had several sons among whom to divide up a massive array of kingdoms, duchies and counties. He seemed incapable of realising that by denying them sufficient independent authority once they passed into manhood, he was creating the rod with which they would beat him when his disenchanted queen goaded them into rebellion.

It was the same with his treatment of Becket, who was almost certainly an infuriating old pedant whose stubborn simple faith was standing in the way of the Church working harmoniously with the State. But Henry was interested only in blind obedience, and his terrifying anger when learning of yet another act of mulish intransigence by his former ally was almost certainly the inspirational cause of Becket's grisly demise. But if ever a man worked devotedly towards martyrdom, it was Thomas Becket.

There were many complex factors at play during this period, which I hope have emerged as you read the previous pages. Chief among these was the fact that England remained only one territory over which the Plantagenet monarchs ruled, and they did not necessarily see it as the centre of their dynastic universe. The Capetian Kings of France had an influence over English foreign policy far greater than their limited landholding might have justified, and we find, throughout this period, that the Kings of England spent what to Englishmen must have seemed like an inordinate amount of time in places such as Normandy, Aquitaine and Poitou, defending other portions of their imperial portfolio. But even Henry did better than the son who succeeded him, Richard, of whose ten-year reign only six months were spent in England. His unfortunate obsession with the Third Crusade, and its consequences for an England dominated by his treacherous younger brother John, feature in the next novel in this series, *The Absentee King*.

It is probably unwise for historical novelists to appear to take sides, but given that the main fictional characters in this novel are predominantly in the service of Eleanor, it was perhaps inevitable that she emerged as more of a victim than she probably was. I have probably underplayed the vehemence with which she drove her sons into rebellion, but no doubt they were perfectly capable of motivating themselves, having been held down for so long by a father who had much to give, but gave so little, either in affection or largesse.

I also plead guilty to playing with the strict timeline in places, most notably the delay on Henry's part in doing penance for the murder of Becket. But it accurately reflects the almost certain fact that he only did so in order to retain friends among those, most notably the Pope, in positions of power who could make or break him. He could have grieved privately for the loss of one of the truest friends he'd ever known but, being Henry, it had to be a melodramatic display.

I hope that you are sufficiently encouraged to acquire the next novel in the series, but whether you are or not, I'd love to get feedback from you on this one — or perhaps even a review of it on **Amazon** or **Goodreads**. Or, if you prefer, send your thoughts to me on my author website, **davidfieldauthor.com**.

David

Sapere Books is an exciting new publisher of brilliant fiction and popular history.

To find out more about our latest releases and our monthly bargain books visit our website: **saperebooks.com**

Printed in Great Britain
by Amazon